STOP!

Each Good vs Evil book has two stories —
one blue and one red — but you can read
it many different ways . . .

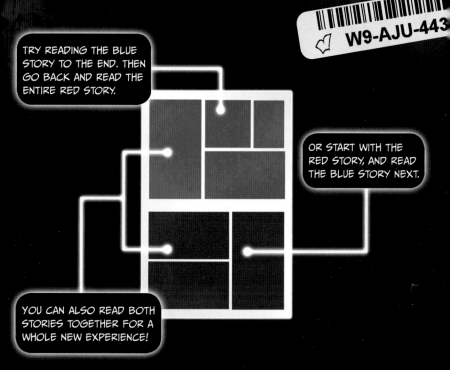

TRY READING THE BLUE
STORY TO THE END. THEN
GO BACK AND READ THE
ENTIRE RED STORY.

OR START WITH THE
RED STORY, AND READ
THE BLUE STORY NEXT.

YOU CAN ALSO READ BOTH
STORIES TOGETHER FOR A
WHOLE NEW EXPERIENCE!

IT'S UP TO YOU!

Read this book again and again to discover exciting,
new details in the neverending battle of . . . Good vs Evil.

THE
AWAKENING

by
Donald Lemke

illustrated by
Claudia Medeliros

STONE ARCH BOOKS
a capstone imprint

Story by Donald Lemke
Illustrated by Claudia Medeliros
Color by Glass House Graphics
Series Designer: Brann Garvey
Series Editor: Donald Lemke
Editorial Director: Michael Dahl
Art Director: Bob Lentz
Creative Director: Heather Kindseth

WWW.CAPSTONEPUB.COM

Good vs Evil is published by Stone Arch Books,
151 Good Counsel Drive, P.O. Box 669, Mankato, Minnesota 56002
Copyright © 2012 by Stone Arch Books.

Library of Congress Cataloging-in-Publication Data
Lemke, Donald B.
  The awakening / written by Donald Lemke ; illustrated by Glass House
Graphics.
    p. cm. -- (Good vs. evil)
  ISBN 978-1-4342-2089-9 (library binding)
1. Graphic novels. [1. Graphic novels. 2. Supernatural--Fiction. 3. Good
and evil--Fiction. 4. Toyko--History--20th century--Fiction. 5. Japan--
History--1945-1989--Fiction. 6. Stories without words.] I. Glass House
Graphics. II. Title.
  PZ7.7.L46Aw 2011
  741.5'973--dc2
201000411

Summary: In 1984, a teenager finds a cassette on the streets of Tokyo,
Japan. At home, the teen sticks the mysterious tape into his Walkman
and pushes play. Suddenly, an Oni-like creature awakens deep below
the apartment building. It surfaces, seeking out the irritating music and
chasing the boy to the rooftop, where both their fates will be decided.

PRINTED IN THE UNITED STATES OF AMERICA IN STEVENS POINT, WISCONSIN.
032011 006111WZF11

"THE REVERSE SIDE ALSO HAS A REVERSE SIDE."

—JAPANESE PROVERB

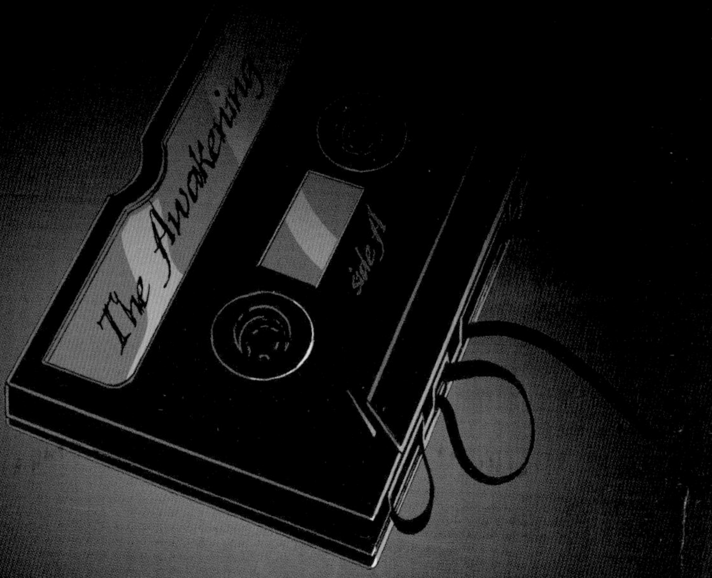
The Awakening
side A

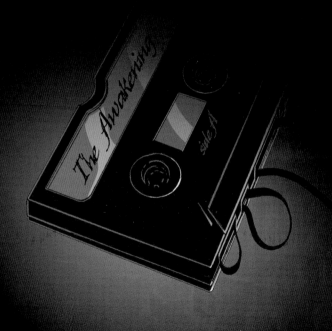

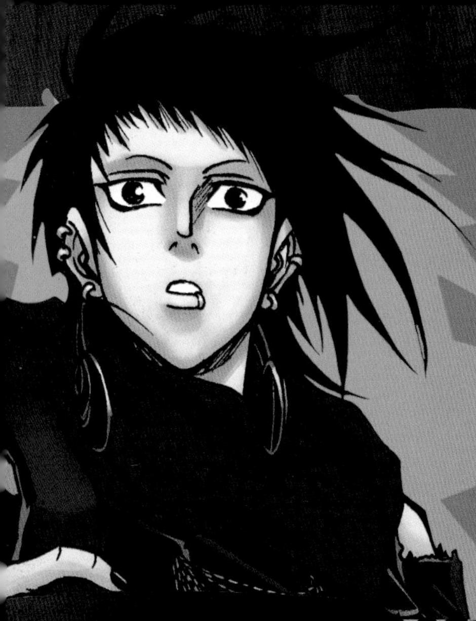

YOSHIRO TANAKA

APRIL 4, 1984, 4:44 PM. YOSHIRO TANAKA STEPS OFF THE SUBWAY AND ONTO THE STREETS OF DOWNTOWN TOKYO, JAPAN. ORPHANED AT AGE FOUR, YOSHIRO HAS BEEN HAUNTED BY DEEP, DARK VOICES EVER SINCE. TONIGHT, HOWEVER, THE TERROR WILL FINALLY END . . .

GOOD VS EVIL

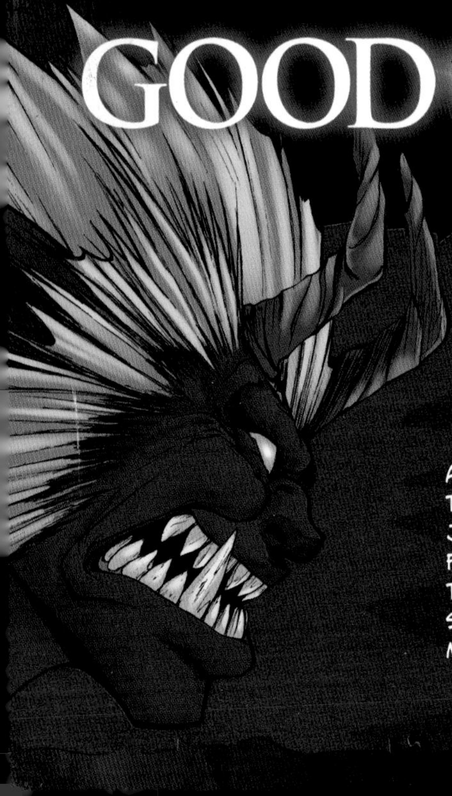

THE ONI

APRIL 4, 1984, 4:44 PM. DEEP BELOW THE DARKENED STREETS OF TOKYO, JAPAN, AN ANGRY CREATURE SLEEPS. FOR MORE THAN ONE HUNDRED YEARS, THE ONI HAS RESTED IN ETERNAL SLUMBER. TONIGHT, HOWEVER, THE MONSTER WILL FINALLY AWAKEN . . .

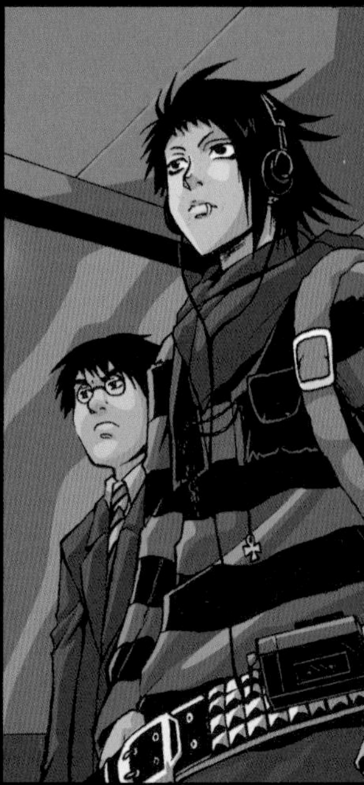

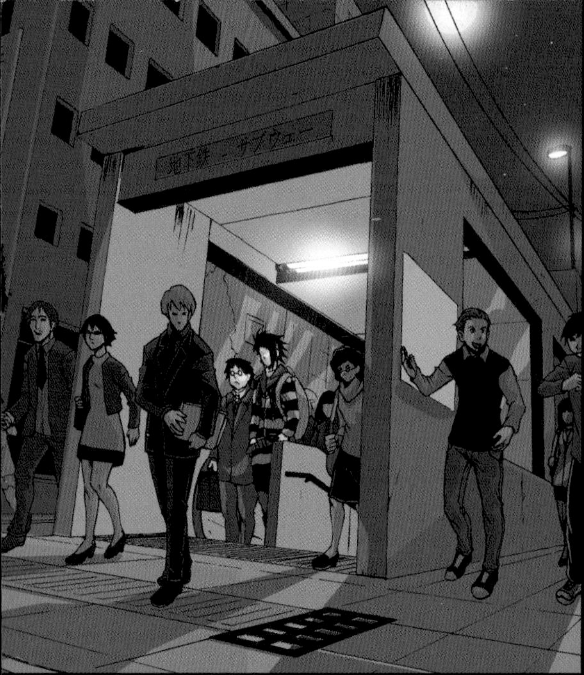
地下鉄 サブウェー

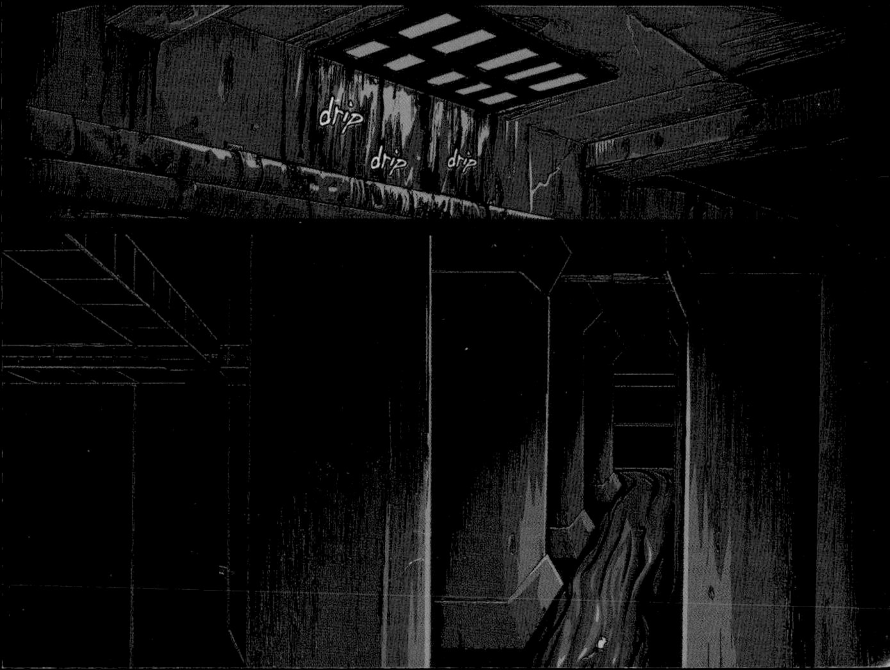
drip
drip
drip

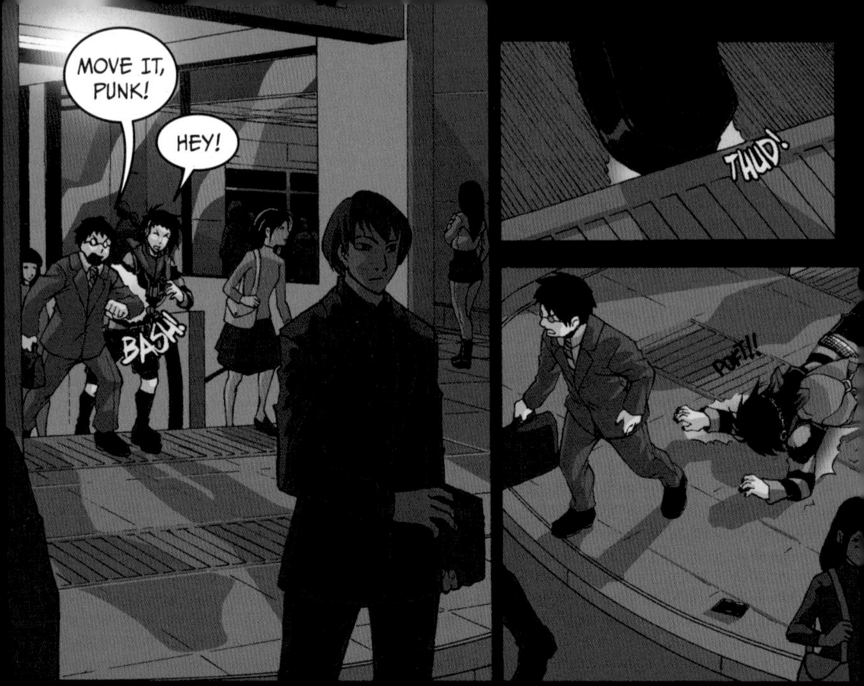
MOVE IT, PUNK!
HEY!
BASH!
THUD!
POFF!!

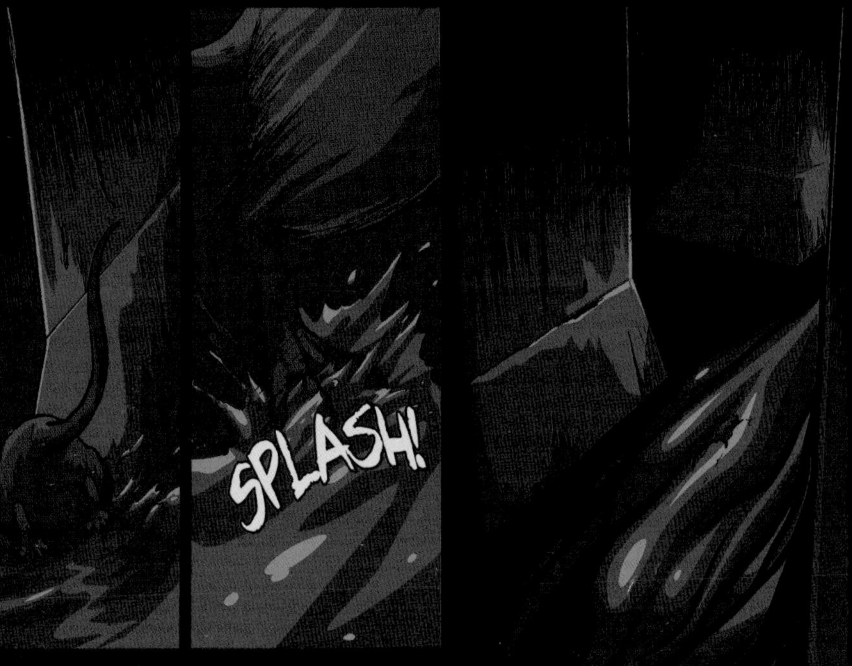
SPLASH!

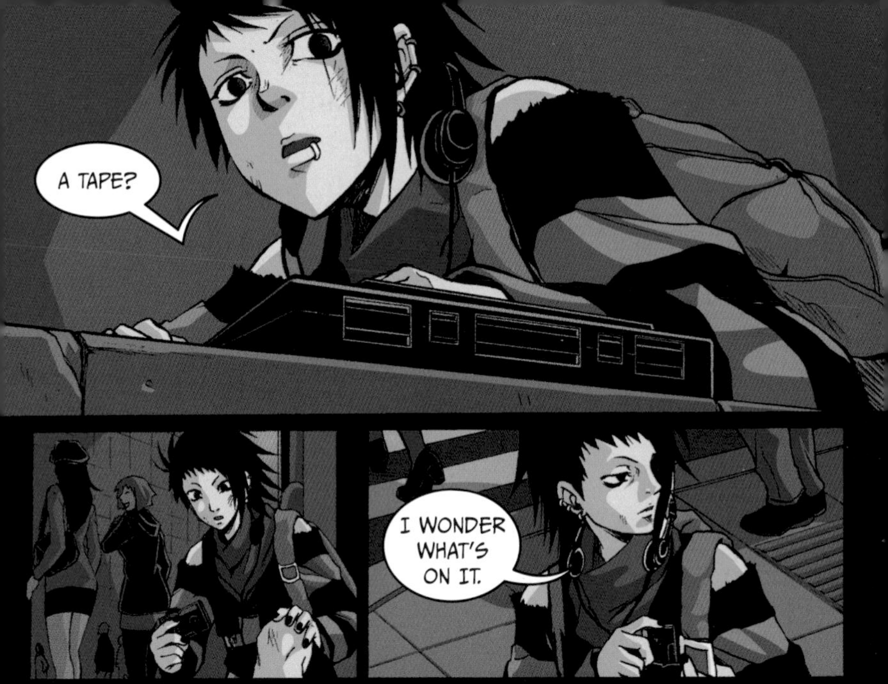
A TAPE?
I WONDER WHAT'S ON IT.

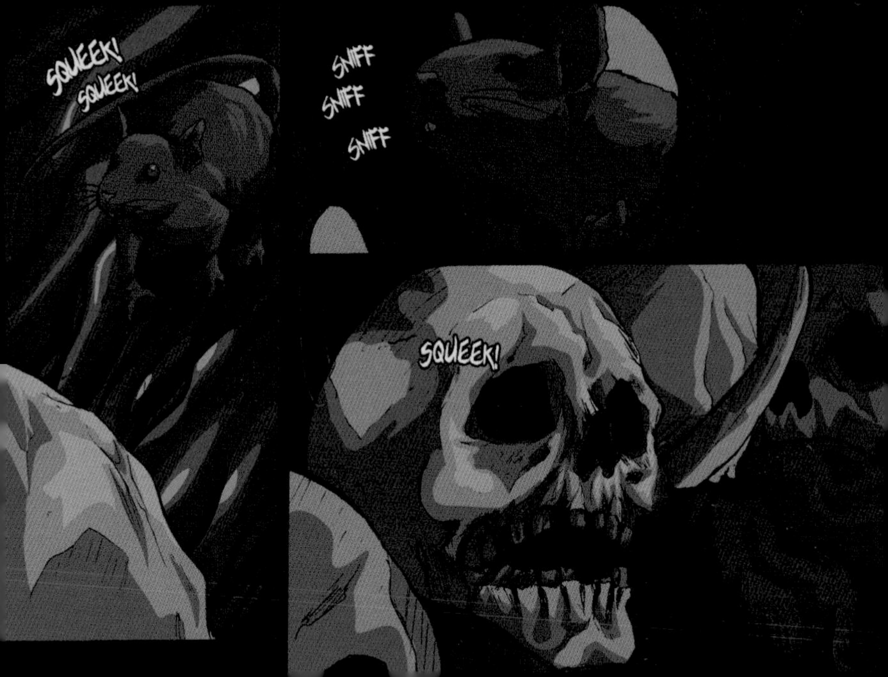
SQUEEK!
SQUEEK!
SNIFF
SNIFF
SNIFF
SQUEEK!

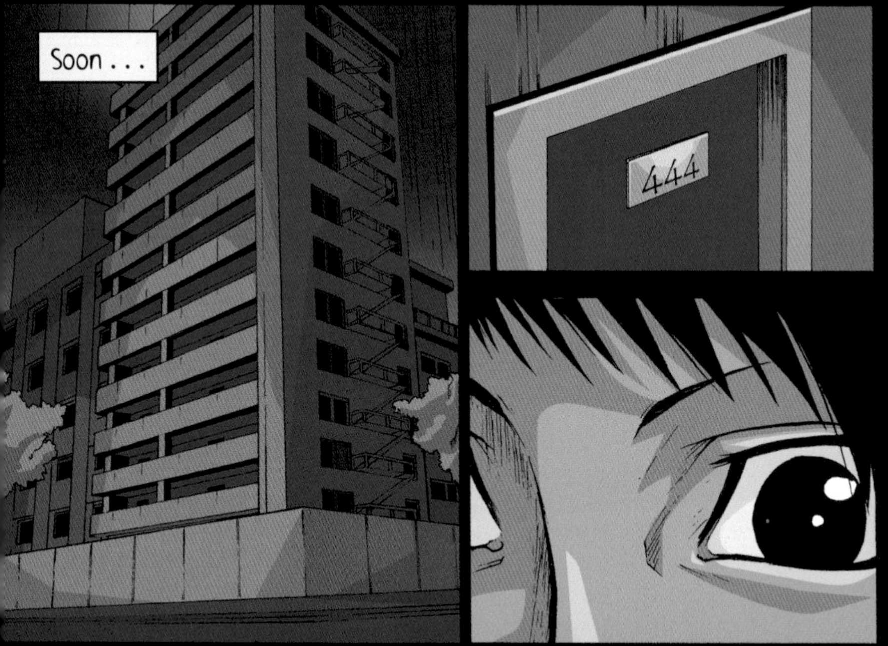
Soon . . .
444

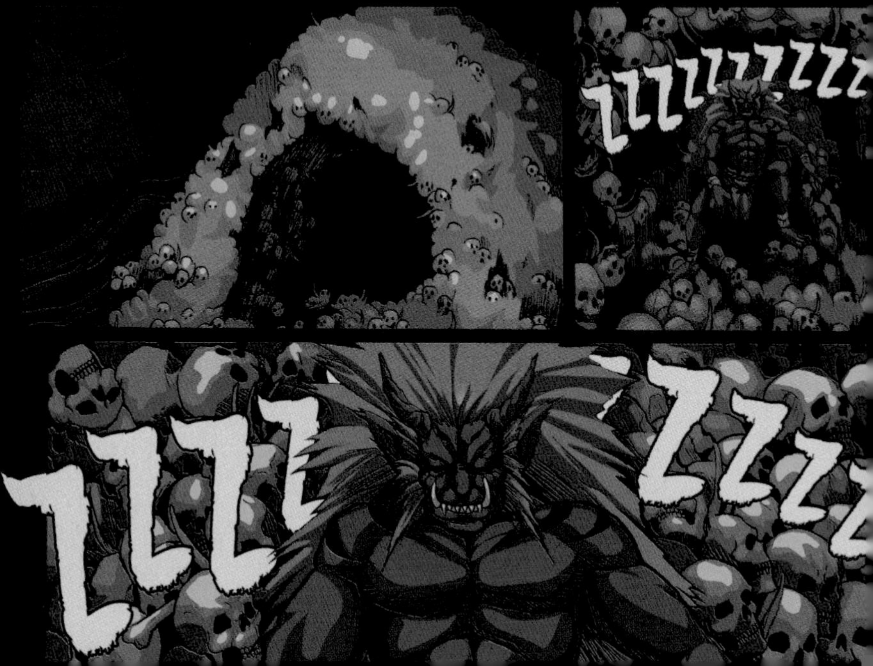
ZZZZZZZZZZ
ZZZZ
ZZZZ

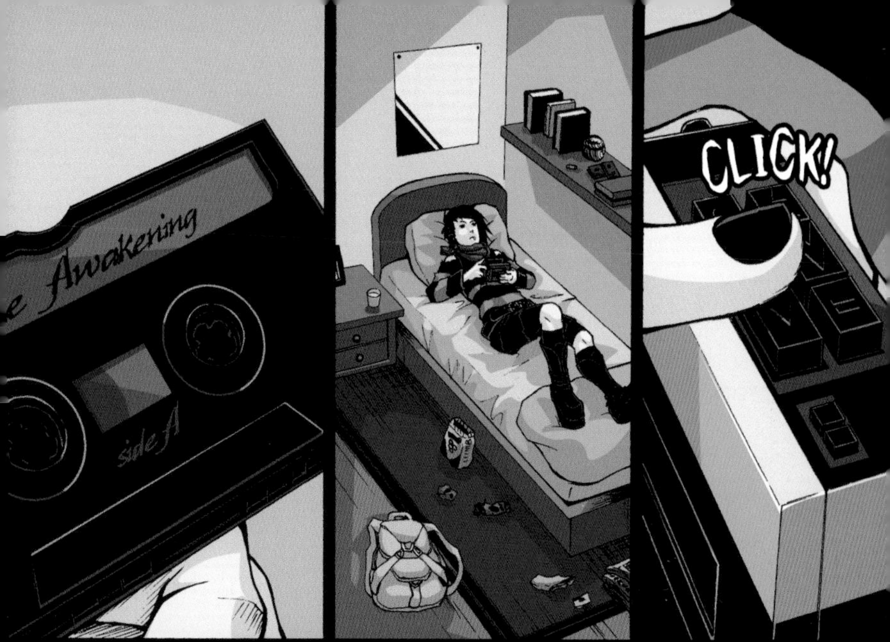
CLICK!
Awakening
side A

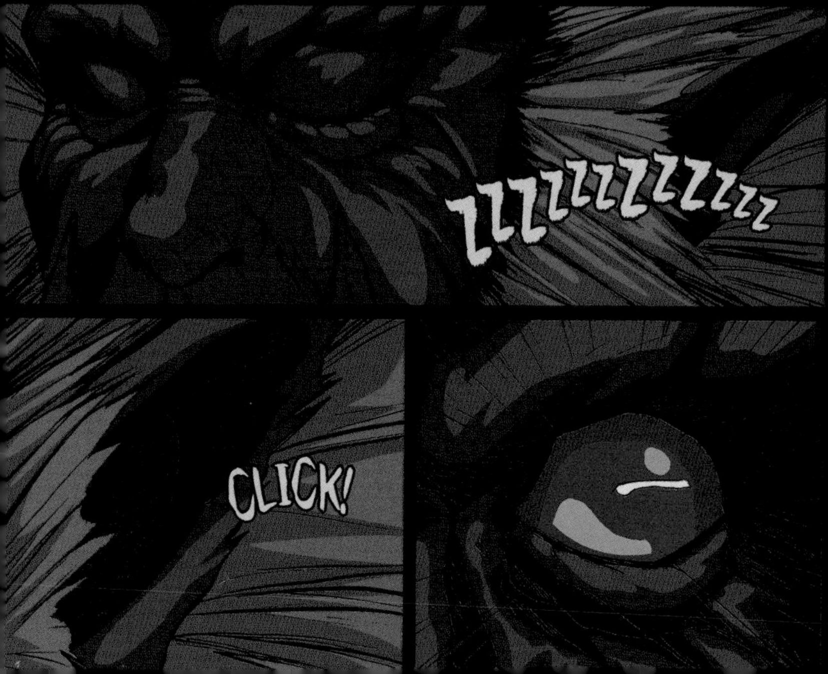
ZZZZZZZZZZZZZ
CLICK!

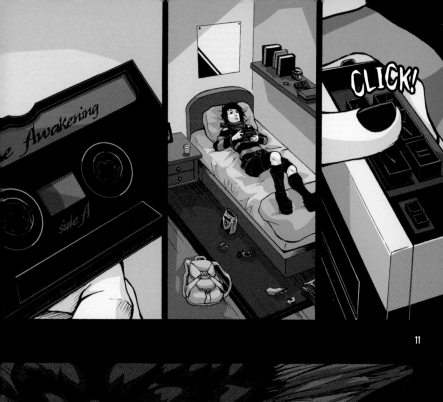

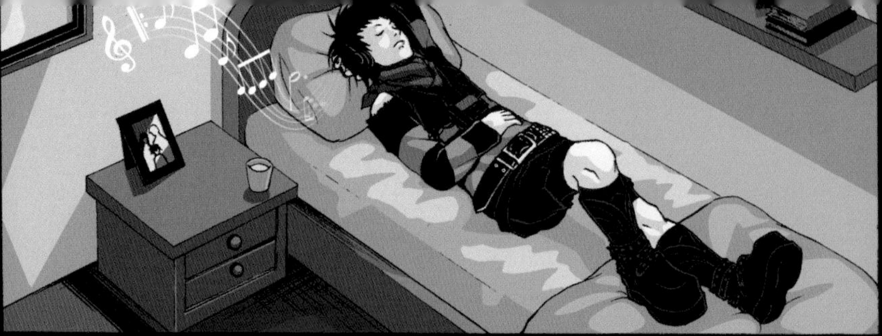

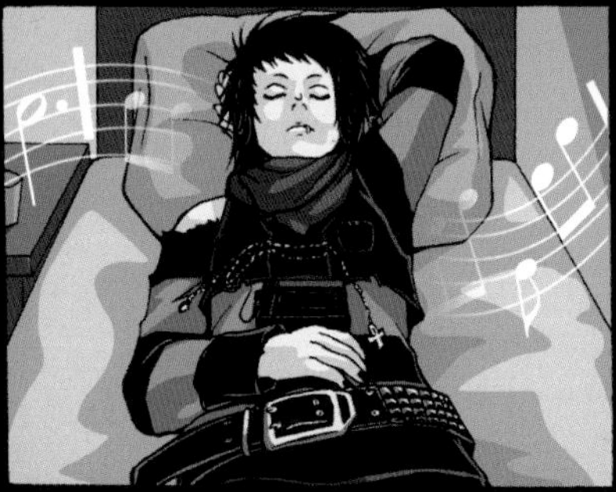

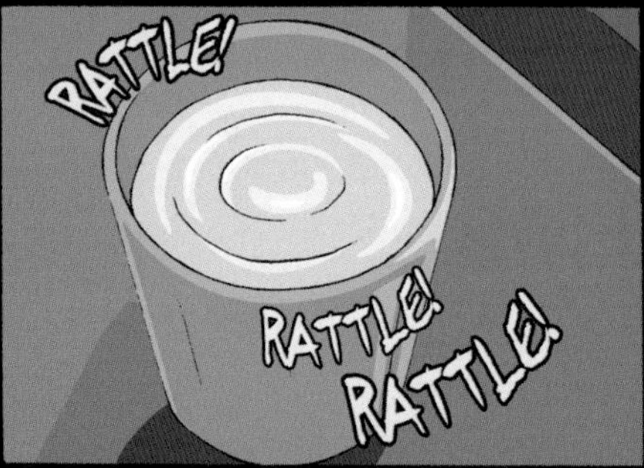
RATTLE!
RATTLE! RATTLE!

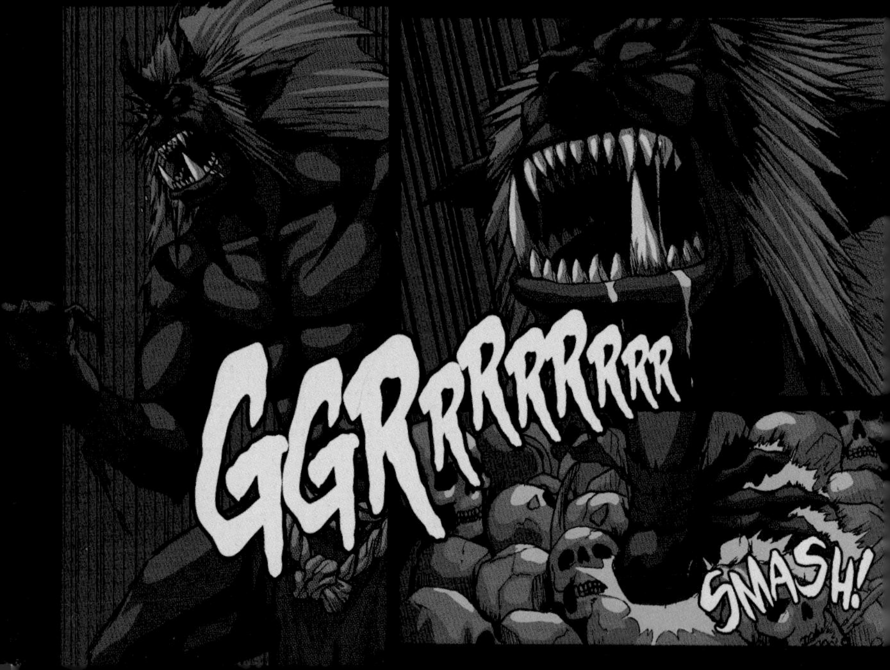
GGRRRRRRRR
SMASH!

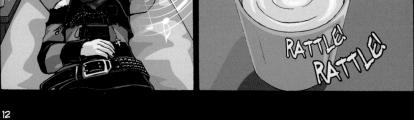

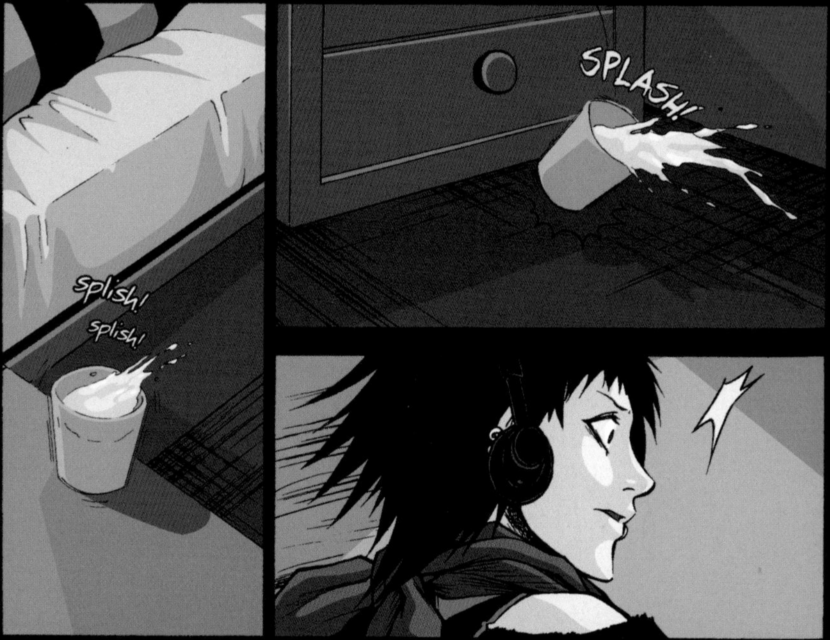
splish!
splish!
SPLASH!

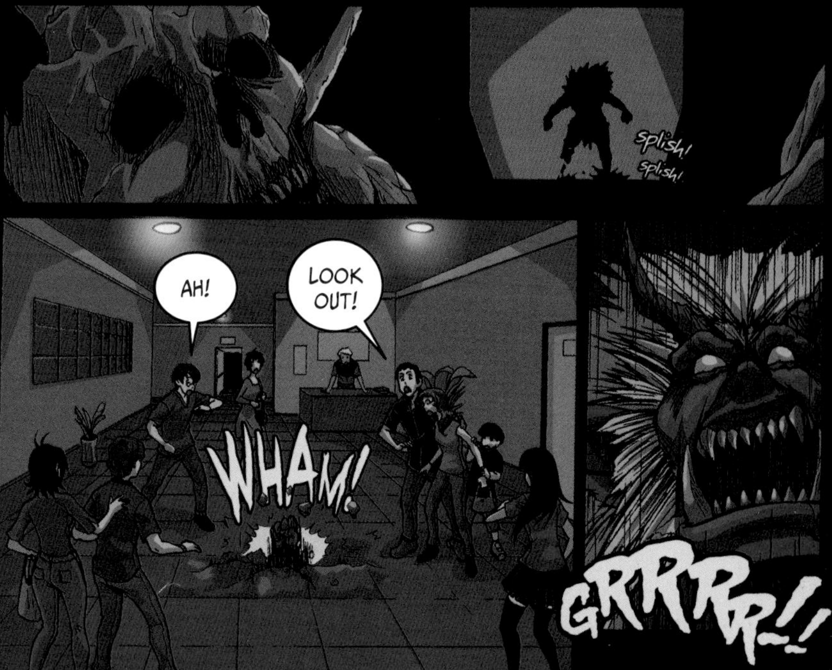
splish!
splish!
AH!
LOOK OUT!
WHAM!
GRRRRR~!!

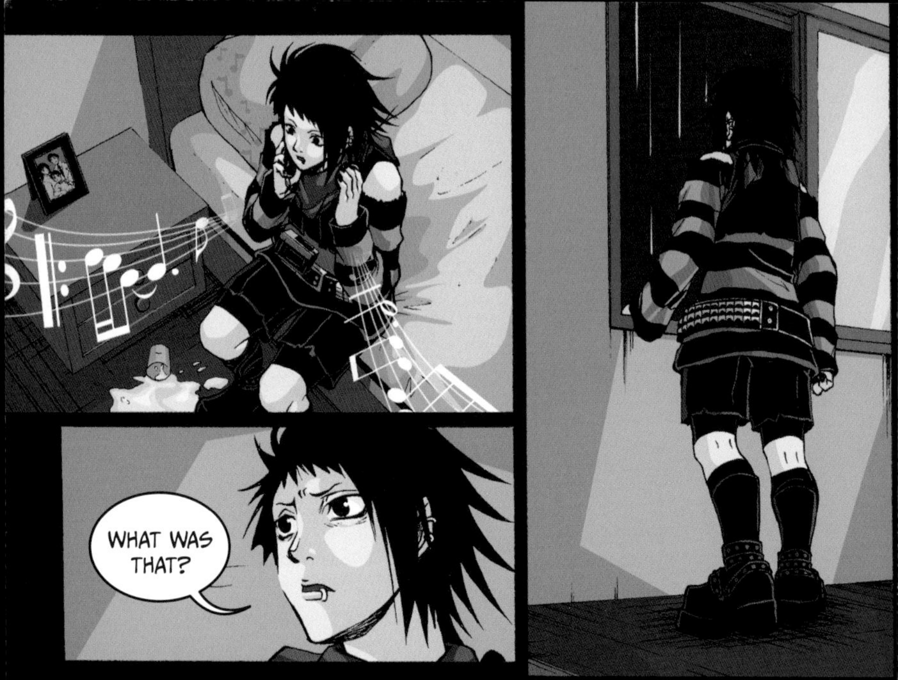
WHAT WAS THAT?

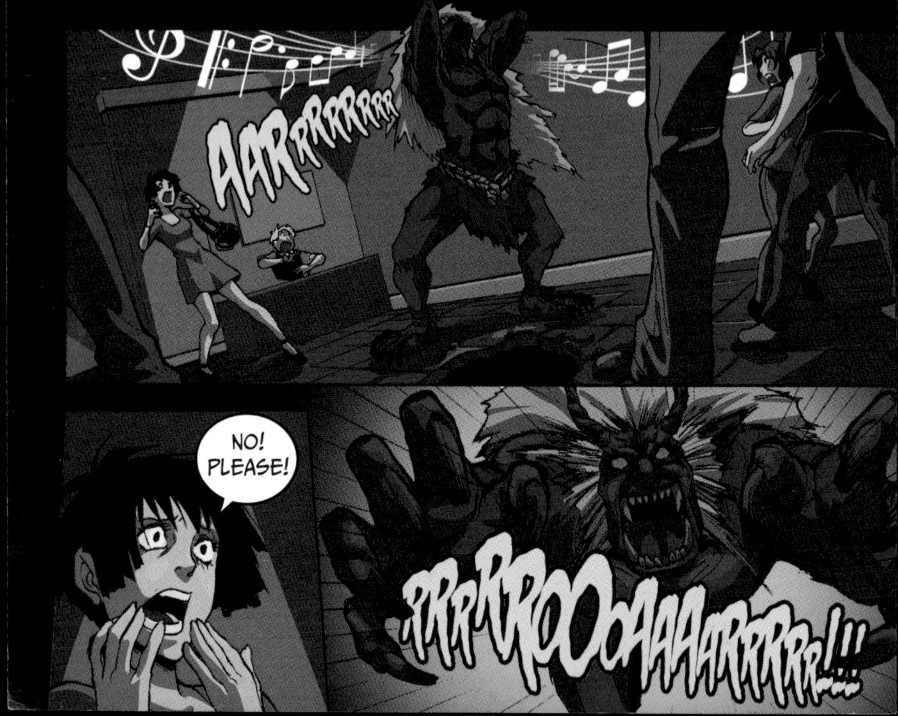
AARRRRRRRR
RRRRROOOAAAARRRRR!!!
NO! PLEASE!

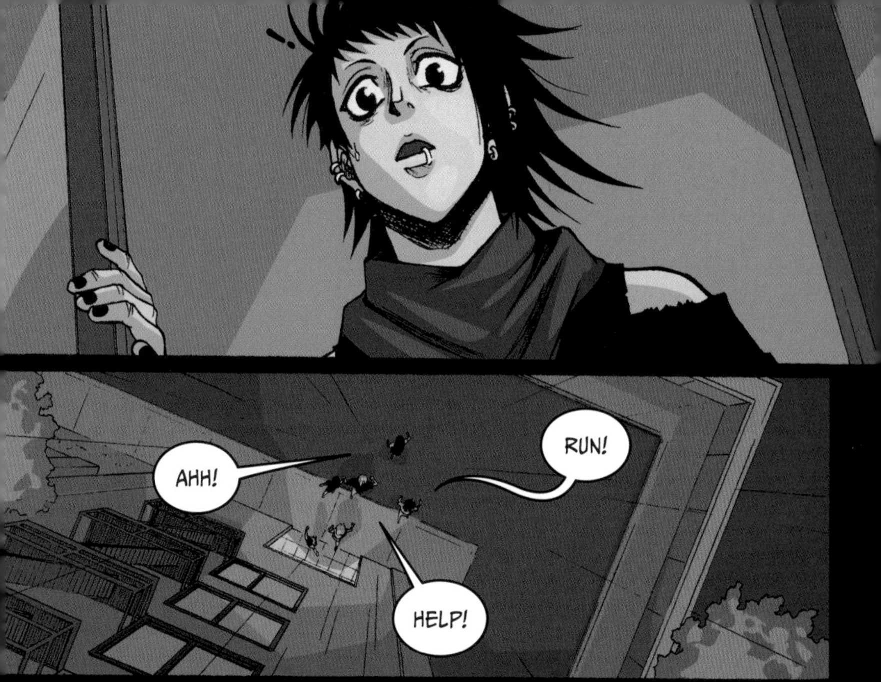
RUN!
AHH!
HELP!

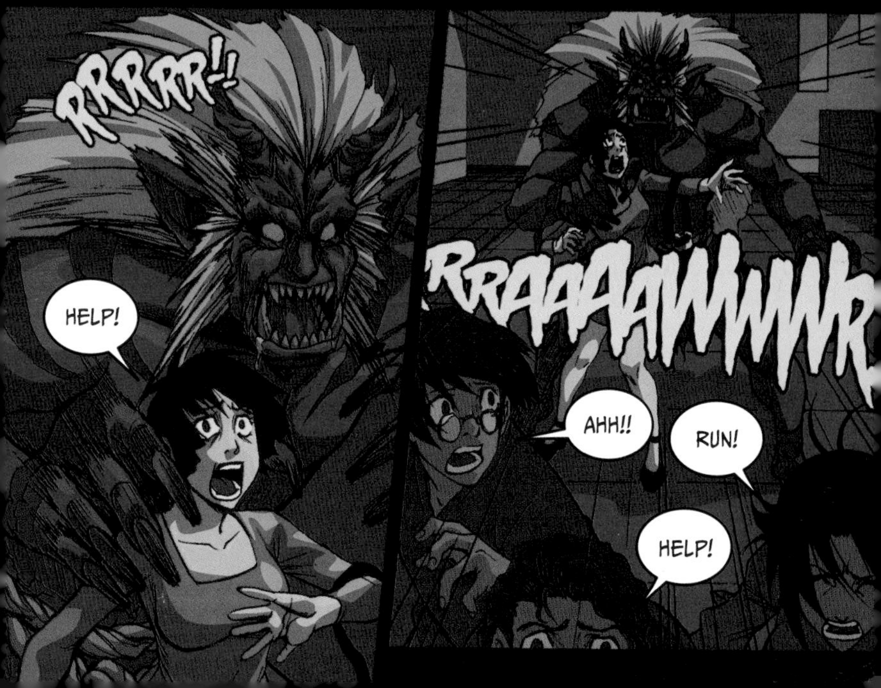
RRAAAAWWWR
AHH!!
RUN!
HELP!
RRRRR!!
HELP!

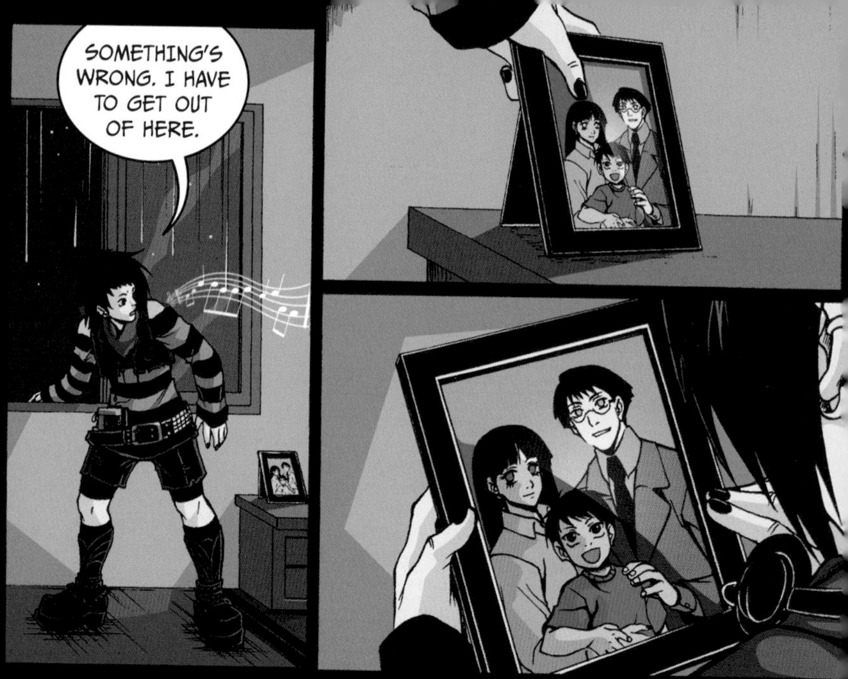
SOMETHING'S WRONG. I HAVE TO GET OUT OF HERE.

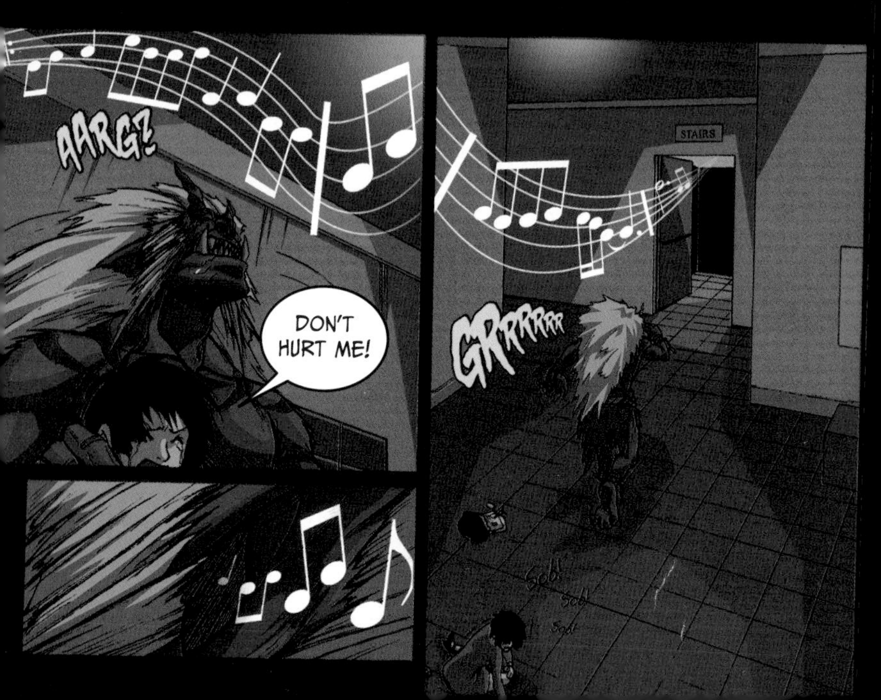
AARG!
DON'T HURT ME!
STAIRS
GRRRRRR
Sob!
Sob!
Sob!

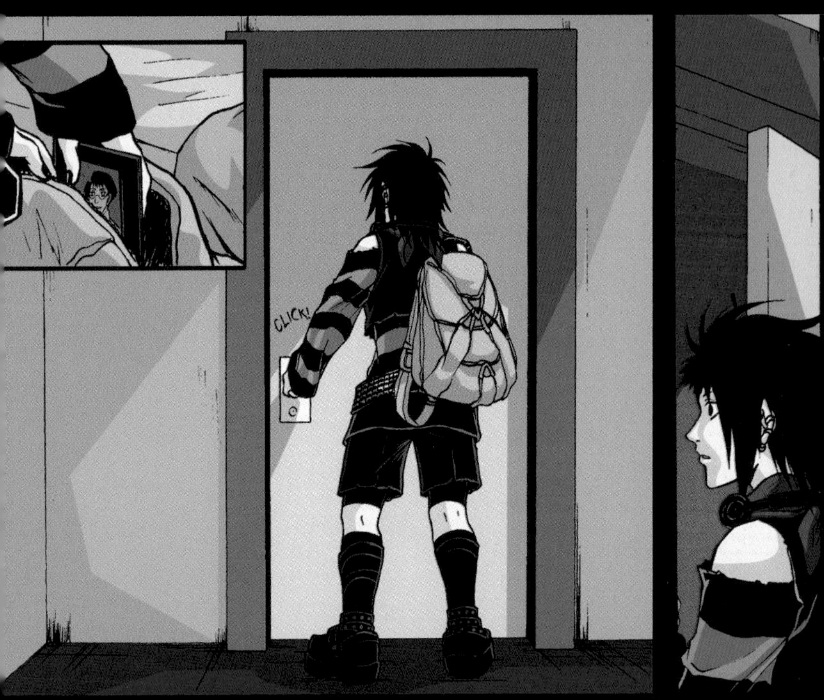
CLICK!

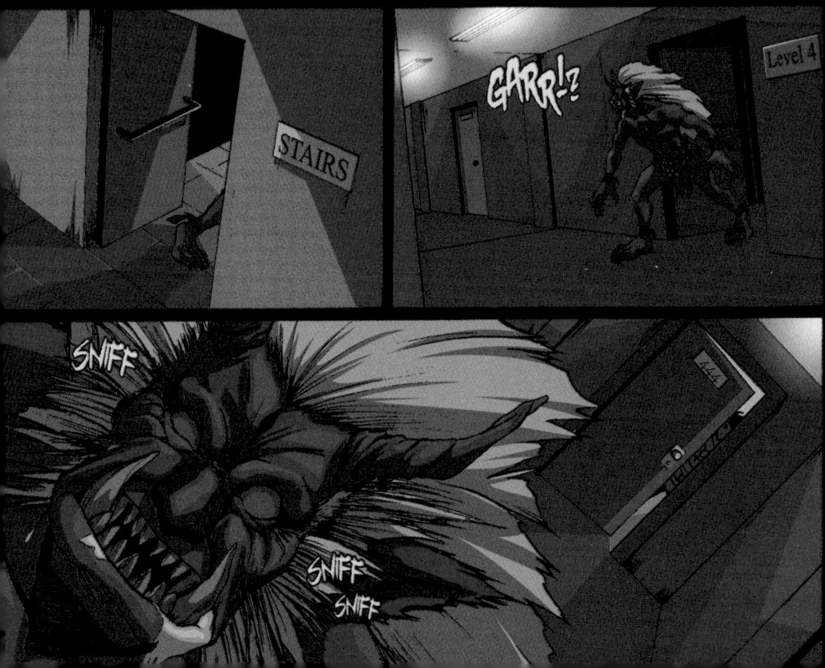
Level 4
GARR!?
STAIRS
SNIFF
SNIFF
SNIFF

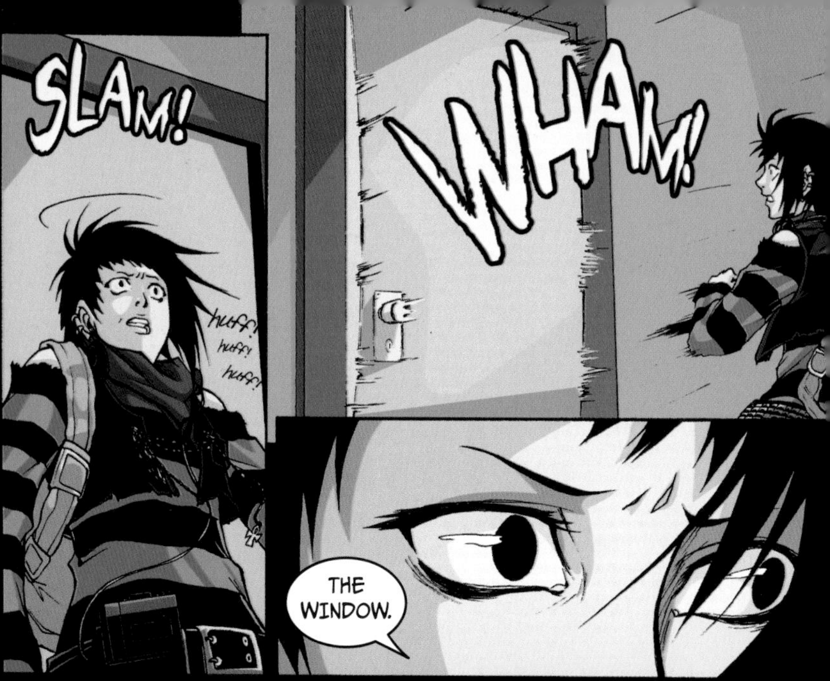
SLAM!
huff!
huff!
huff!
WHAM!
THE WINDOW.

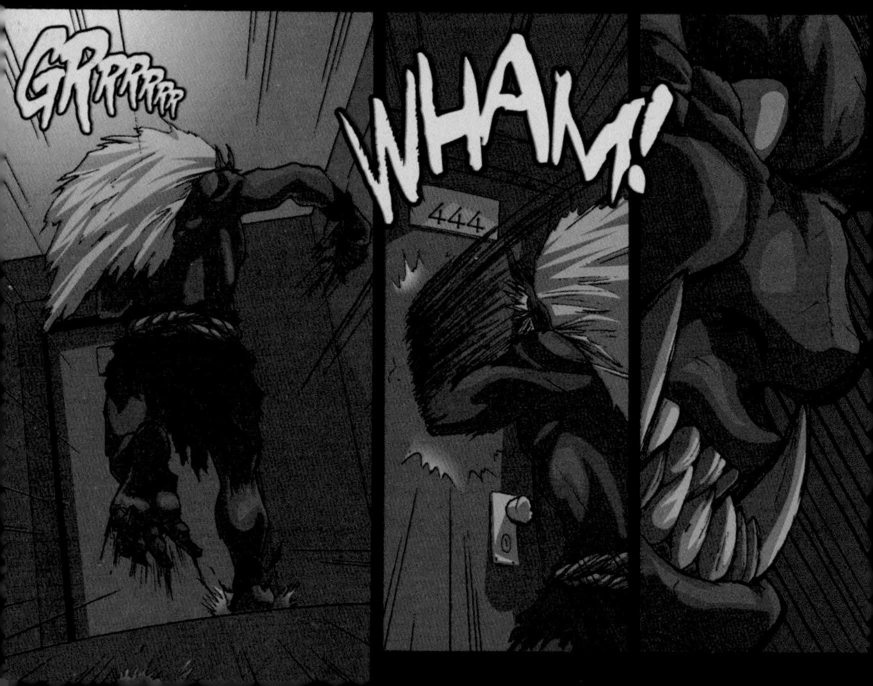
GRRRRRR
WHAM!
444

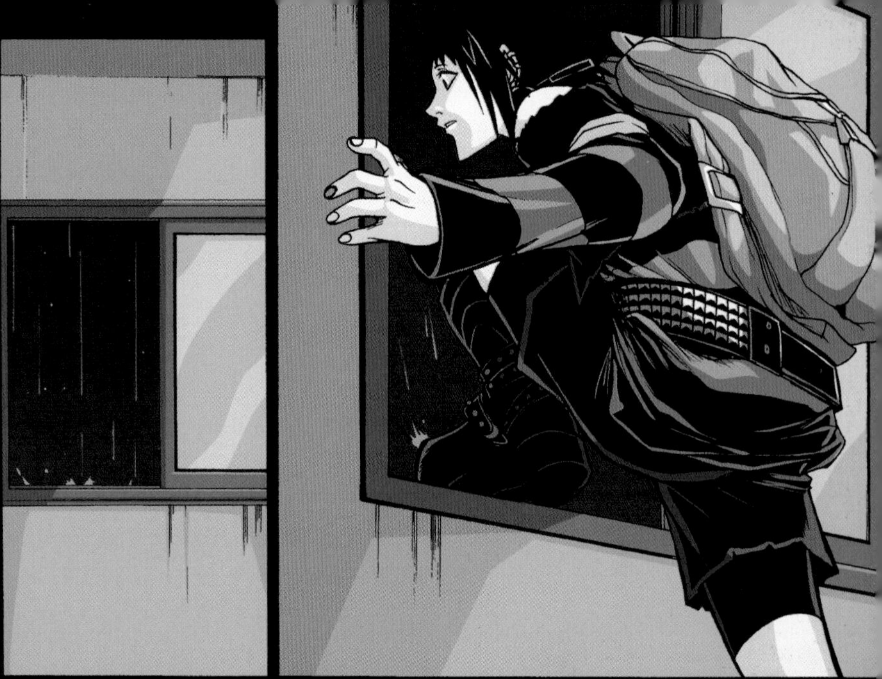

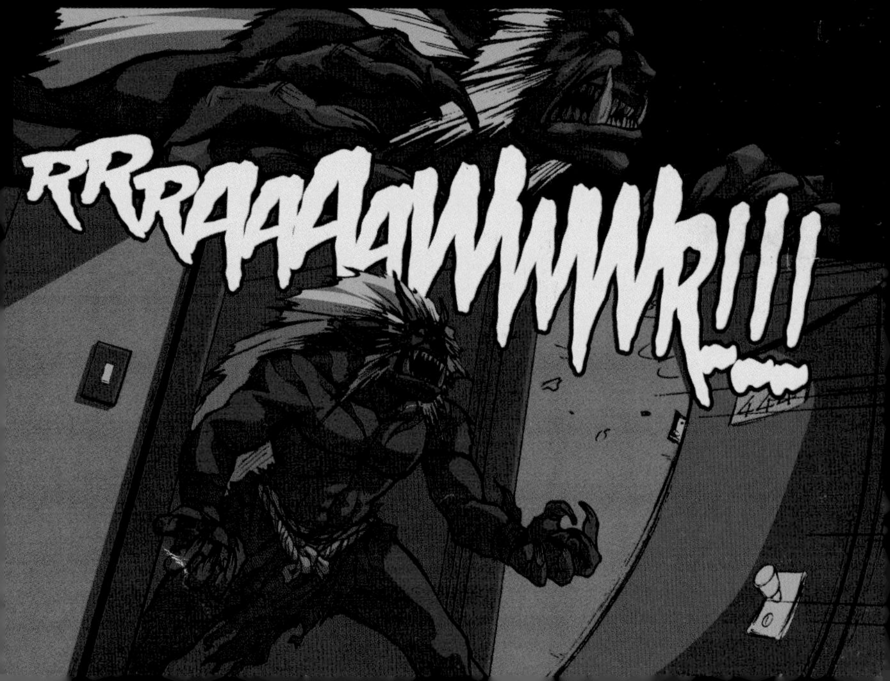
RRRAAAAWWWWR!!!

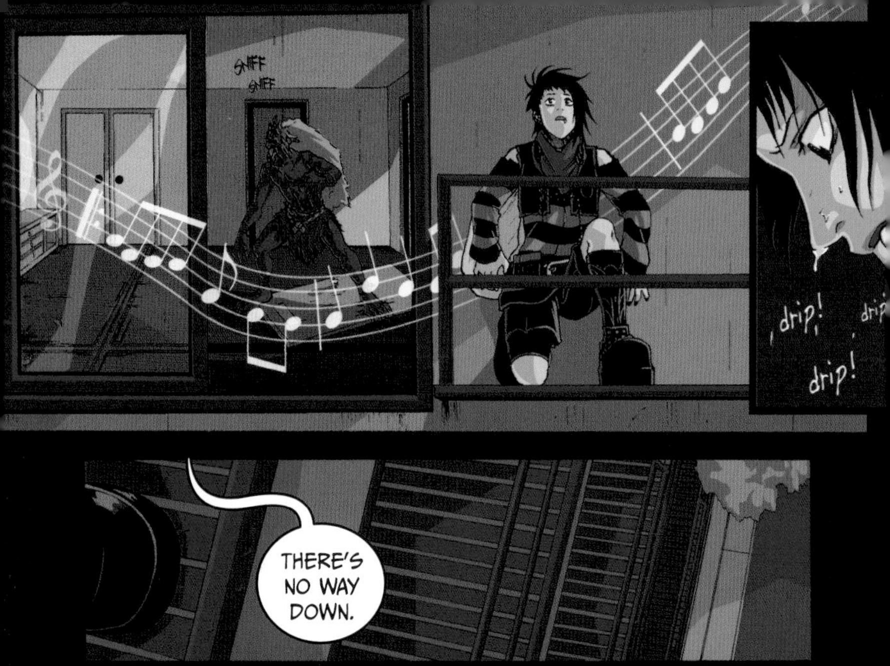
SNIFF
SNIFF
drip!
drip!
drip!
THERE'S NO WAY DOWN.

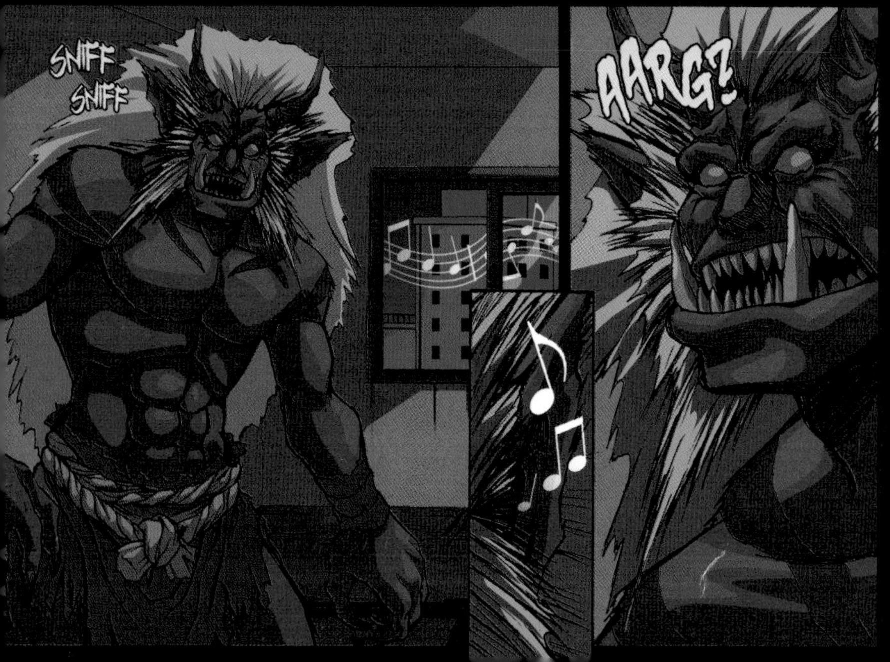
SNIFF
SNIFF
AARG?!

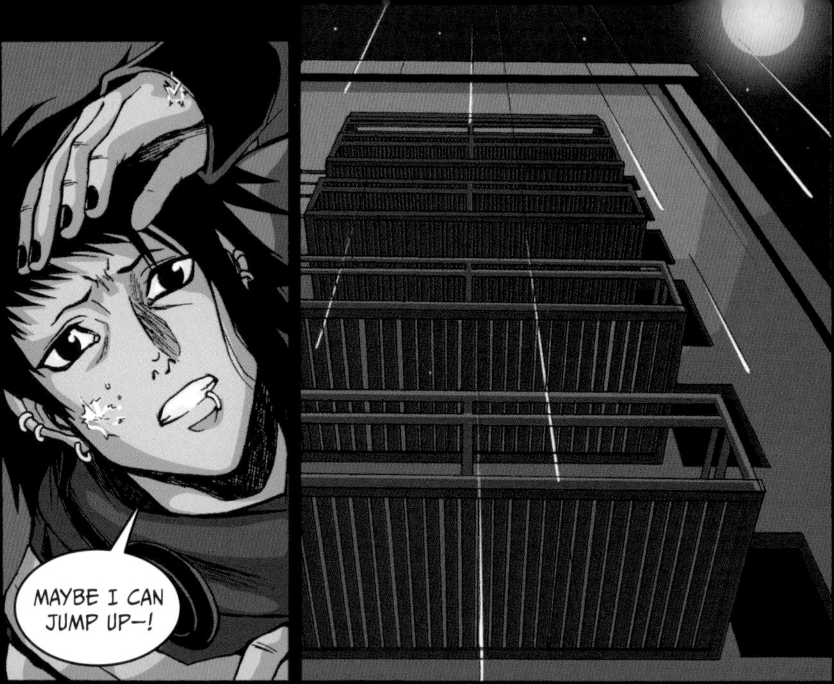
MAYBE I CAN JUMP UP–!

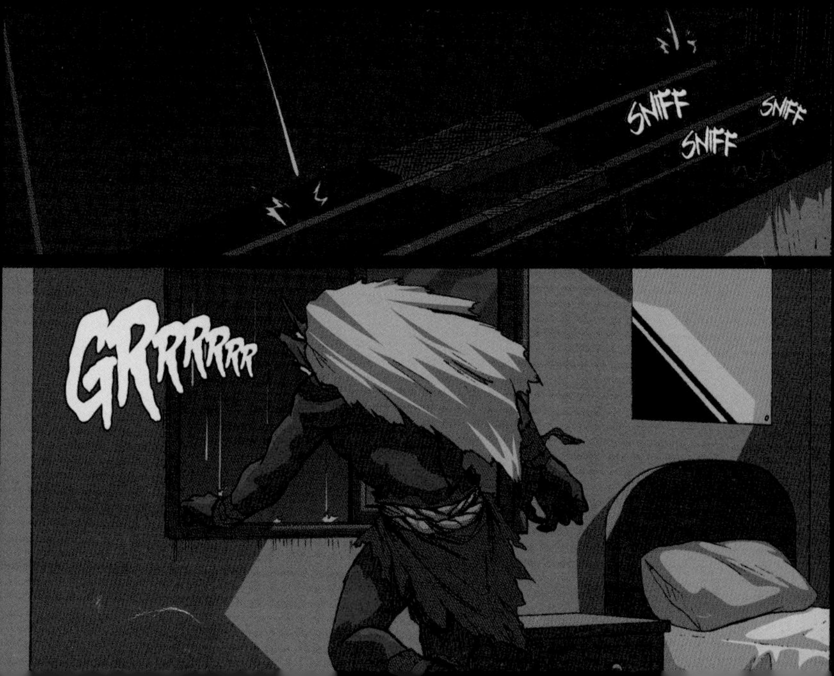
SNIFF
SNIFF
SNIFF
GRRRRRR

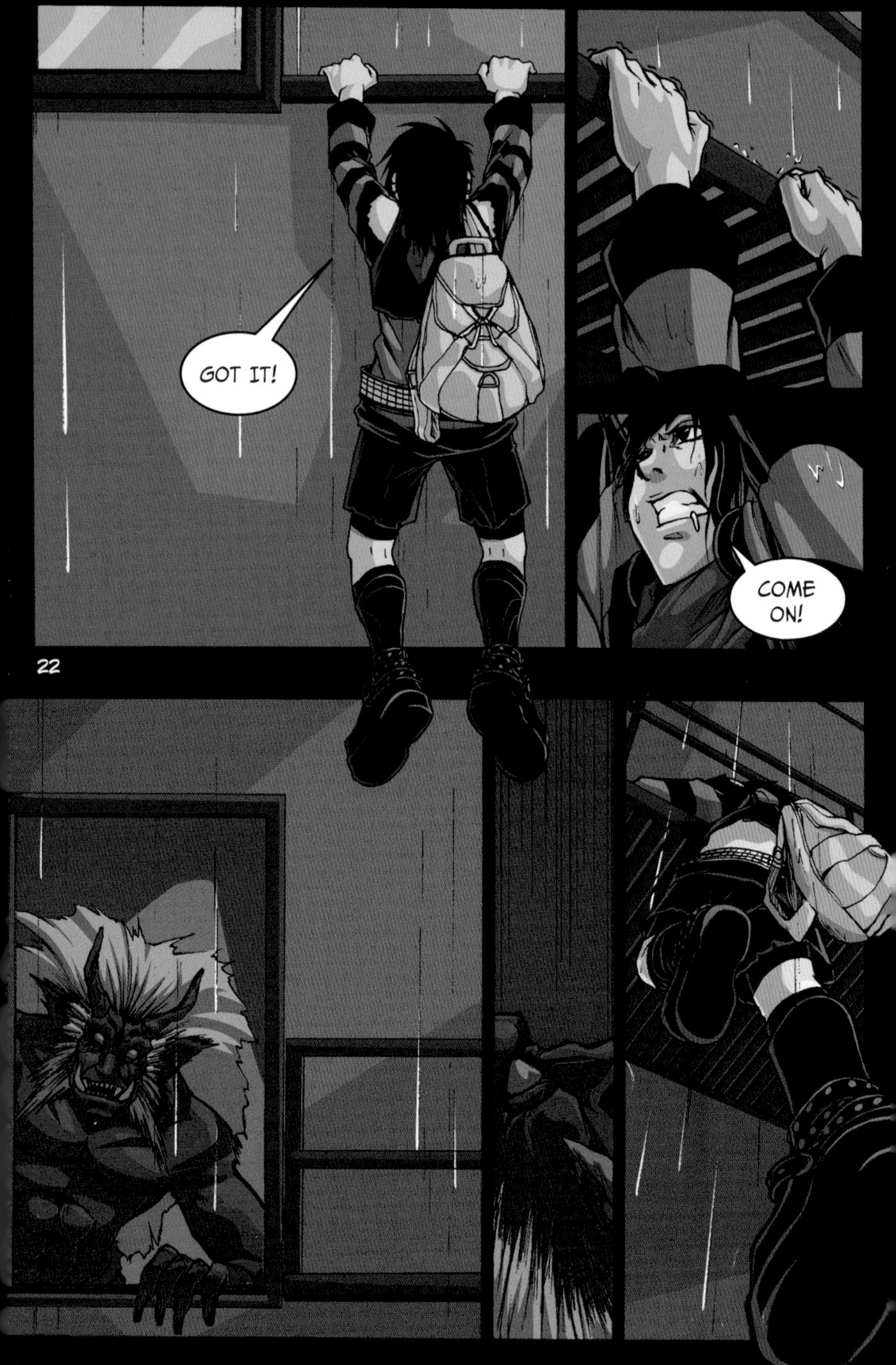
GOT IT!
COME ON!

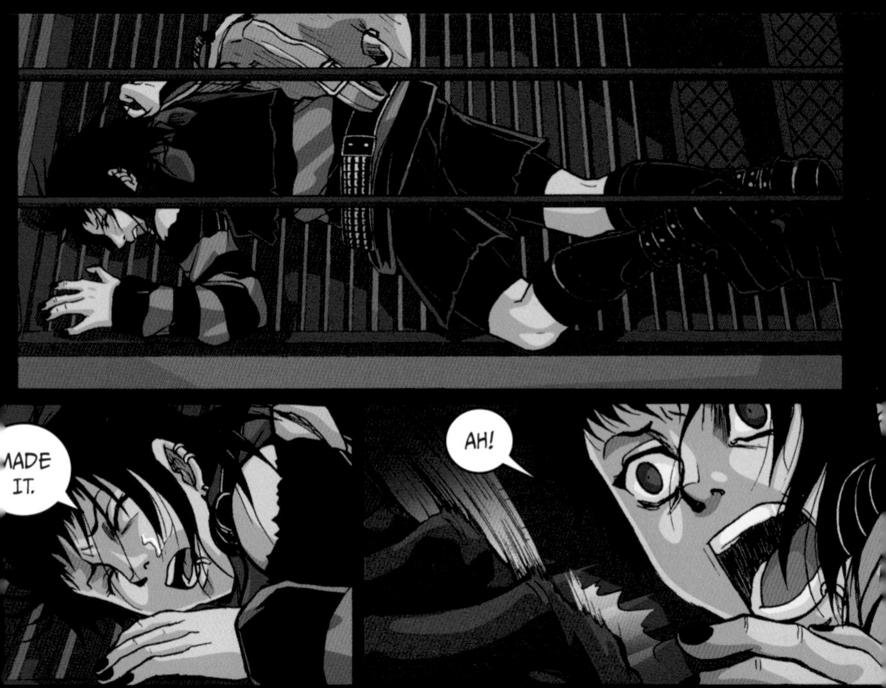
MADE IT.
AH!

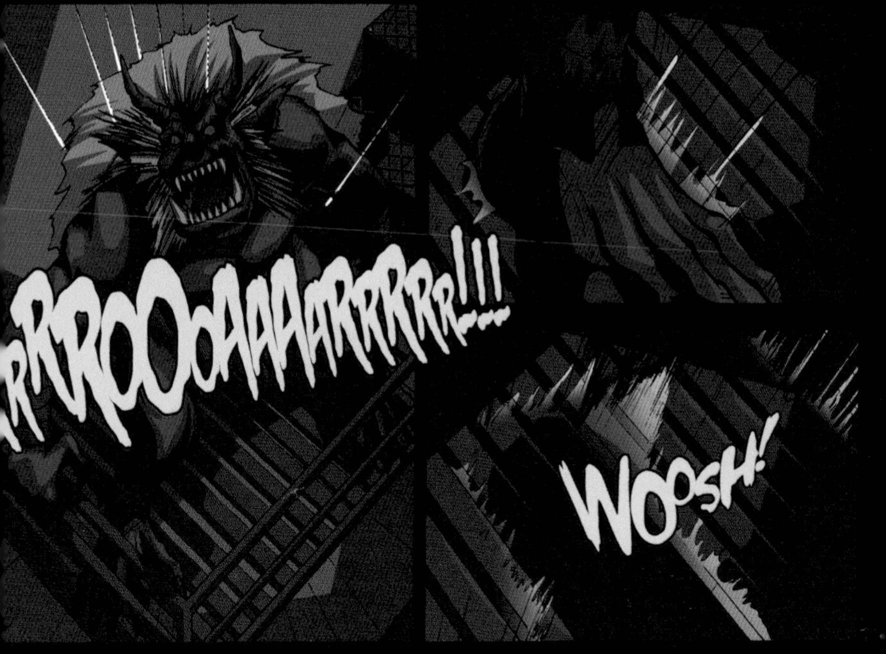
RRROOOAAAARRRRR!!!
WOOSH!

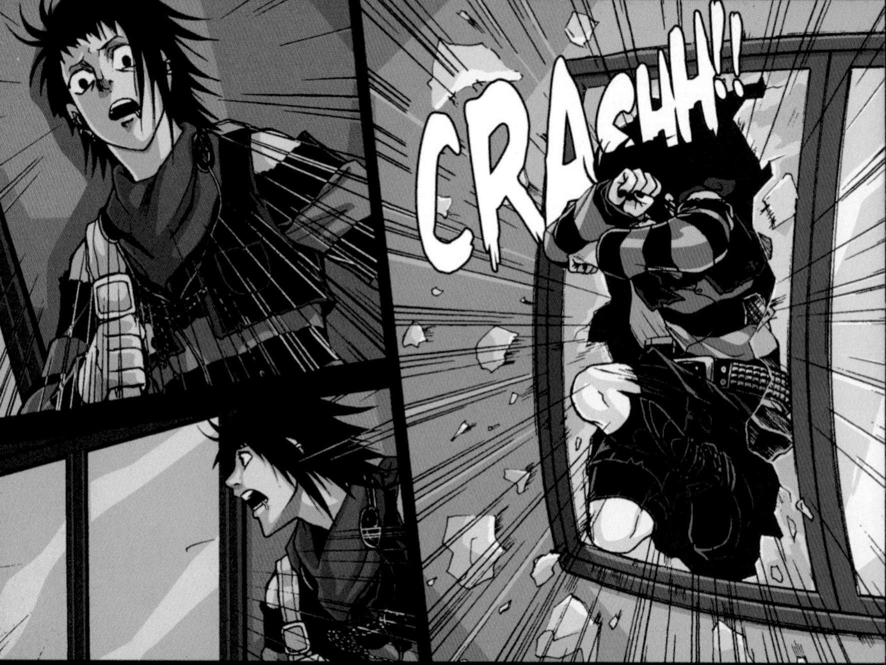
CRASHH!!

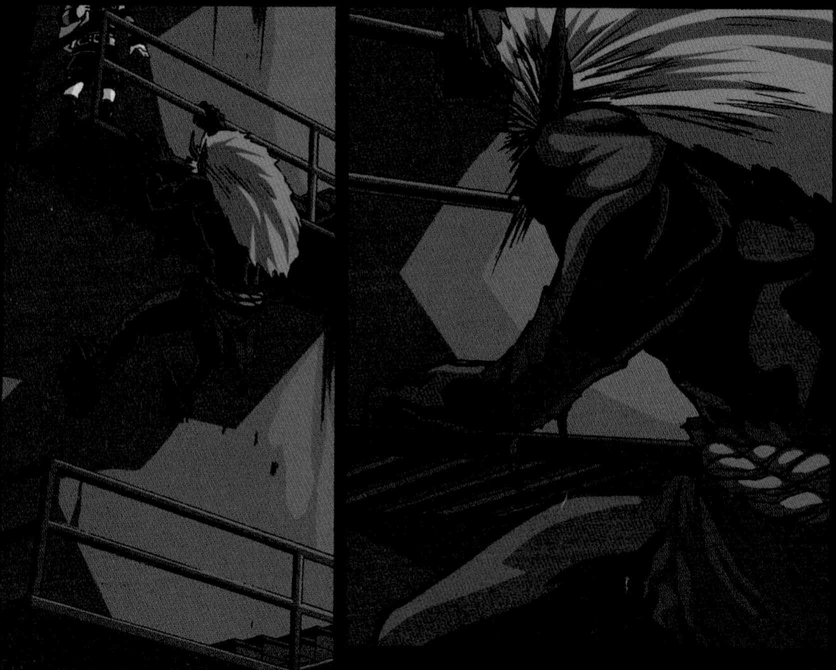

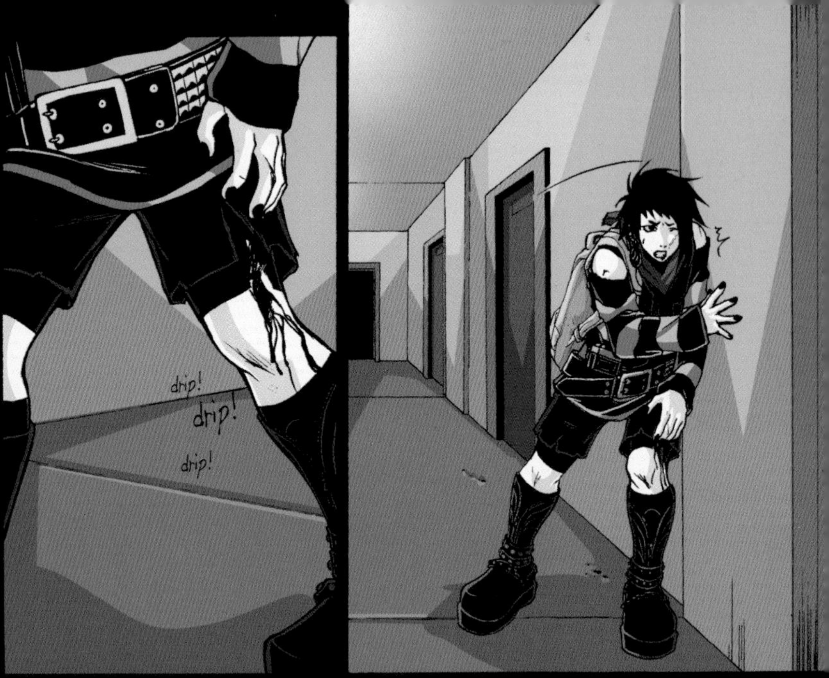
drip!
drip!
drip!

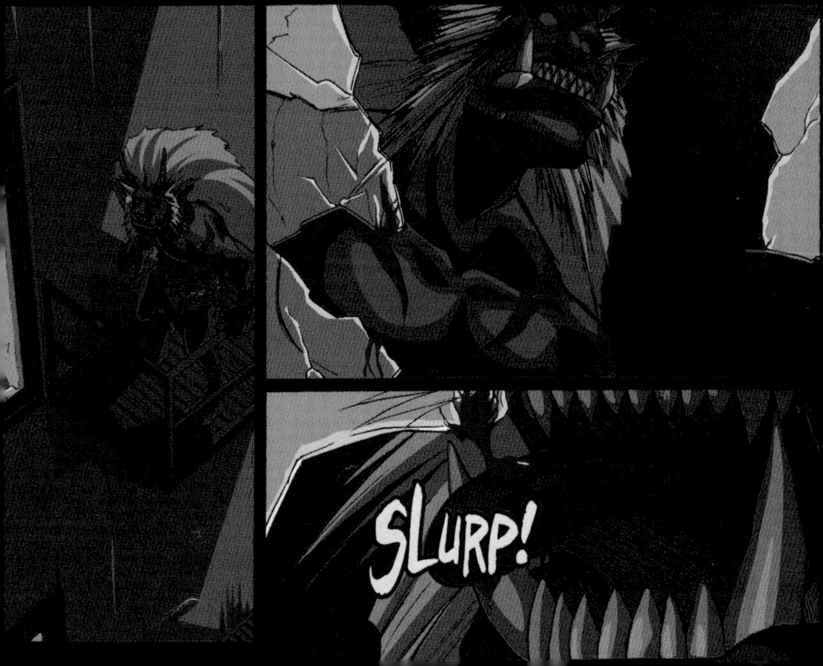
SLURP!

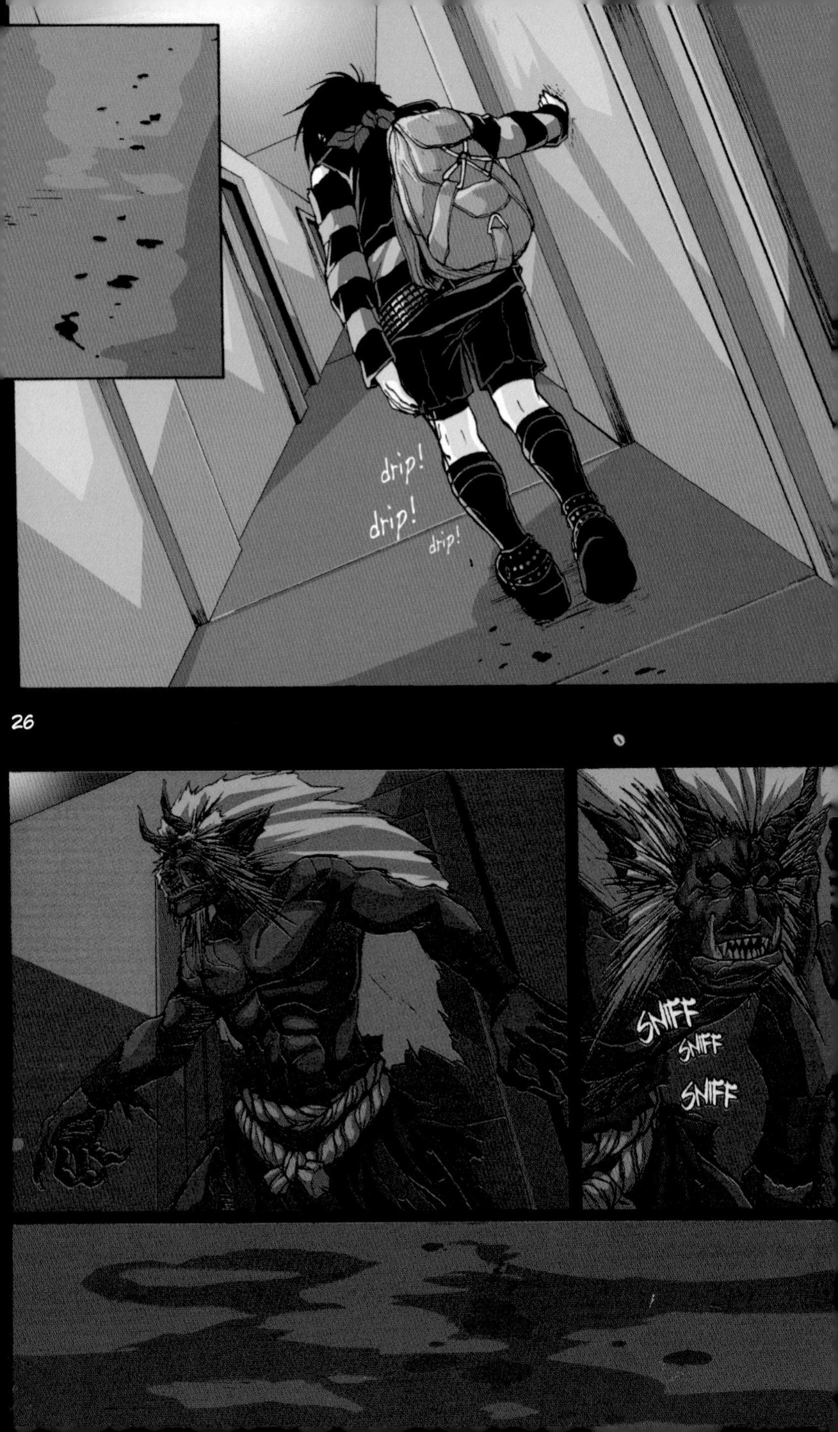
drip!
drip!
drip!
SNIFF
SNIFF
SNIFF

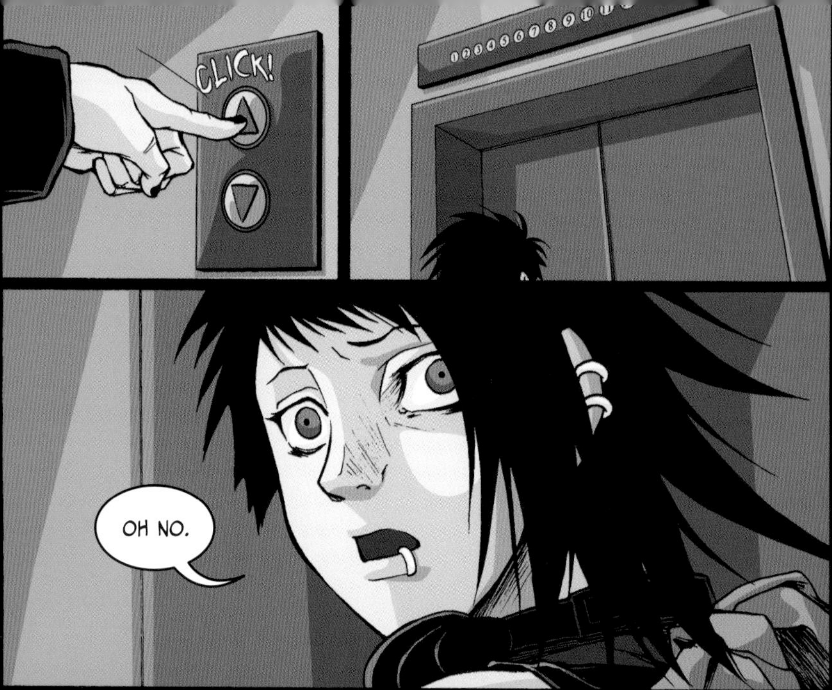
CLICK!
OH NO.

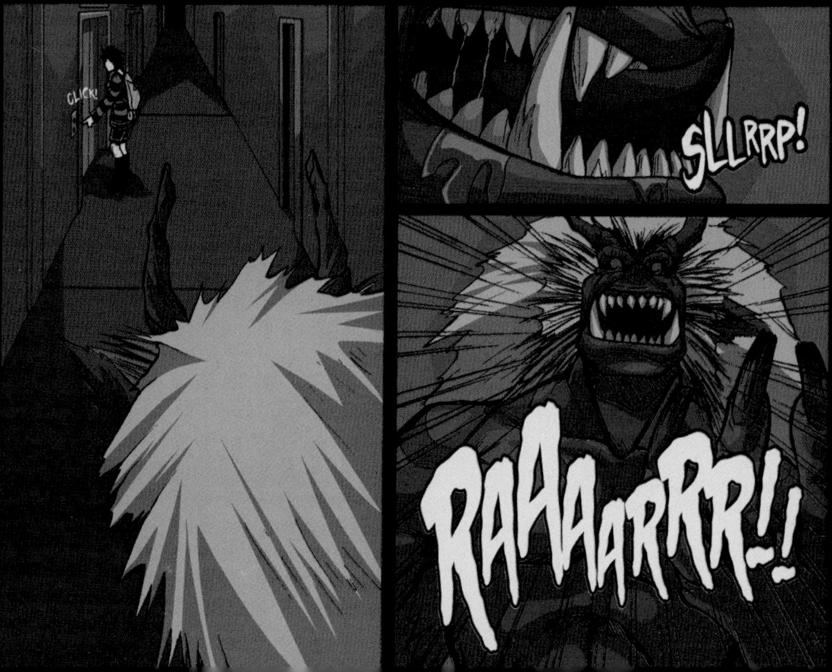
CLICK!
SLLRRP!
RAAAARRR!!

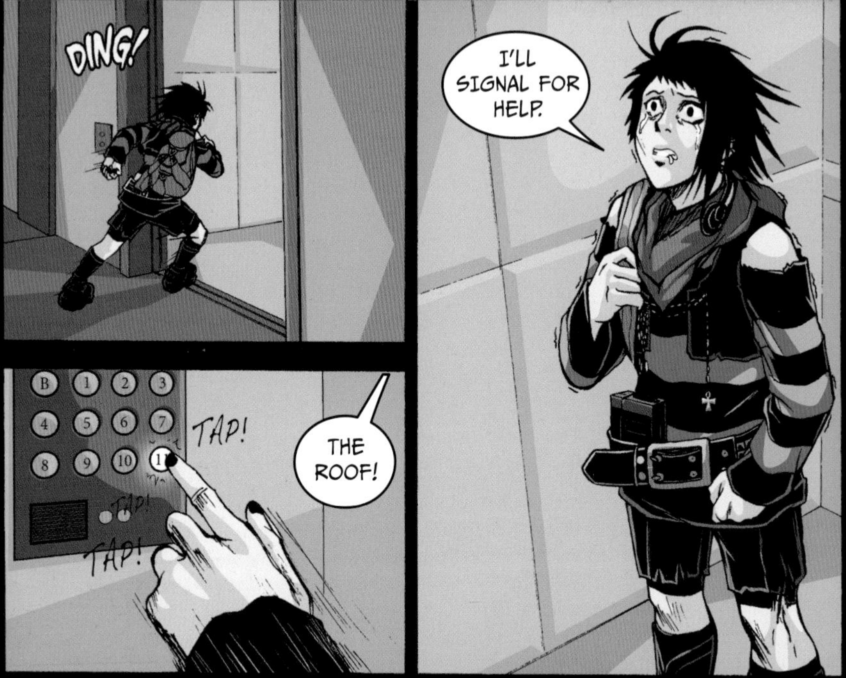
DING!
TAP!
TAP!
TAP!
THE ROOF!
I'LL SIGNAL FOR HELP.

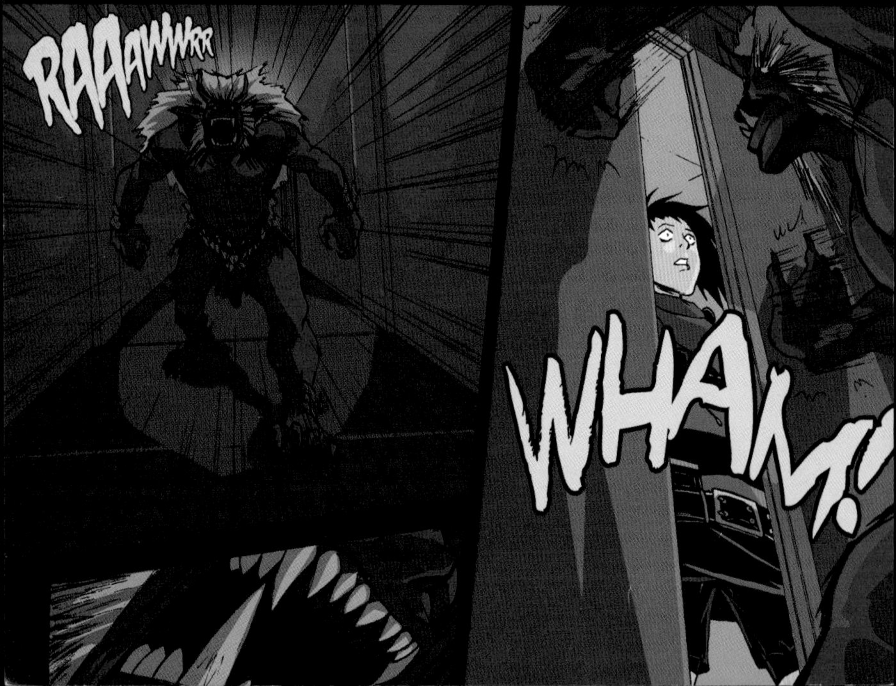
RAAAWWRR
WHAM!

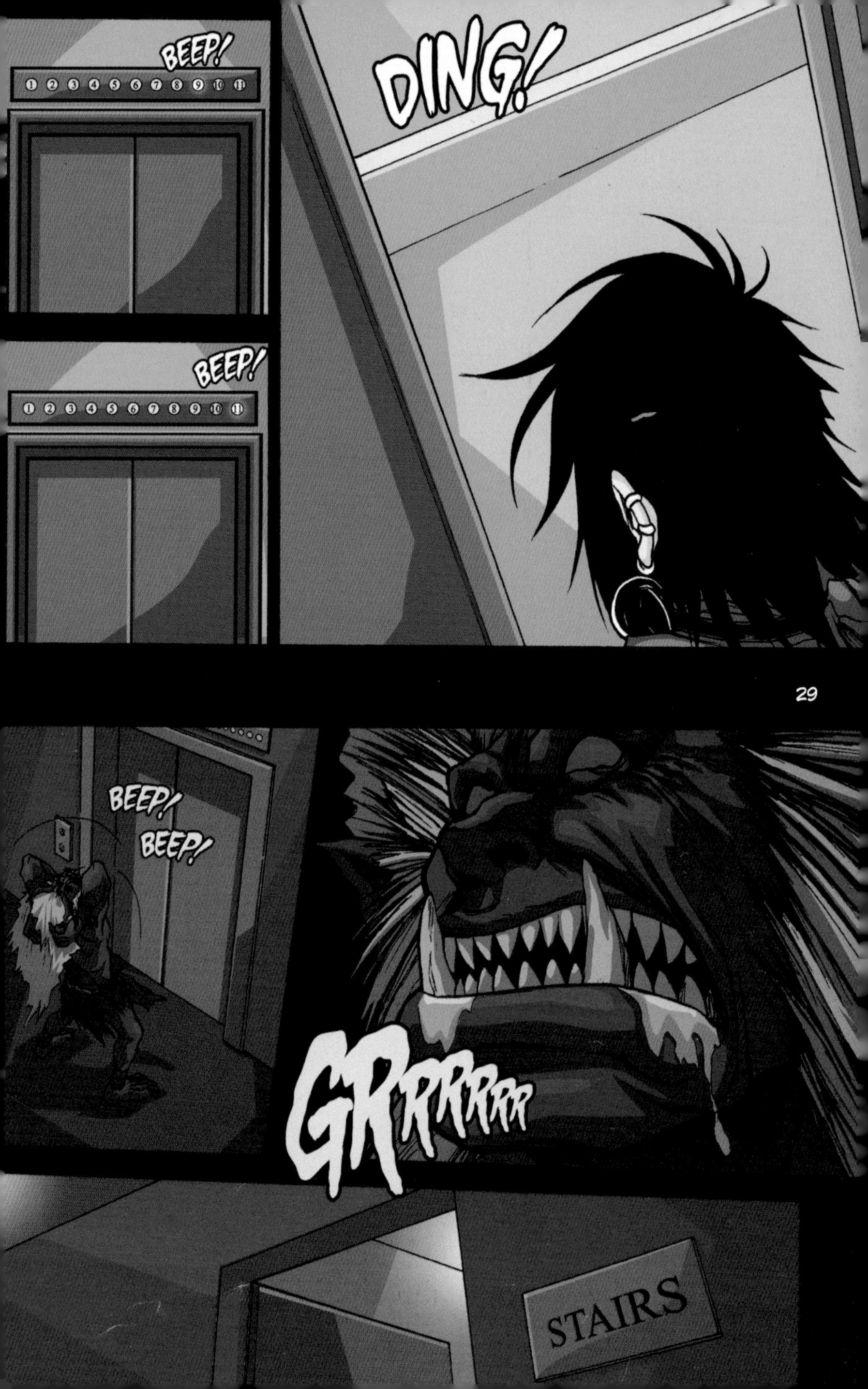
BEEP!
BEEP!
DING!
BEEP!
BEEP!
GRRRRRR
STAIRS

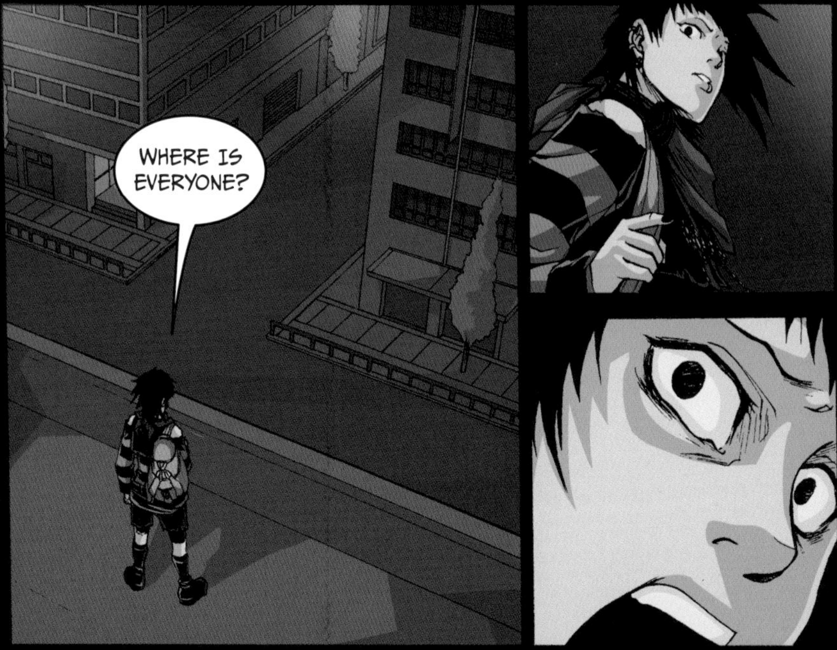
WHERE IS EVERYONE?

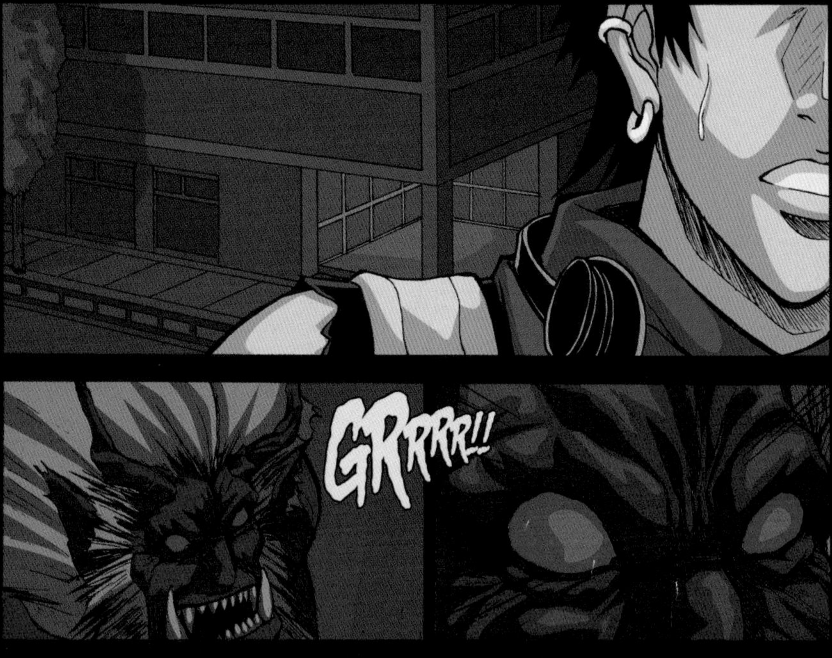
GRRRR!!

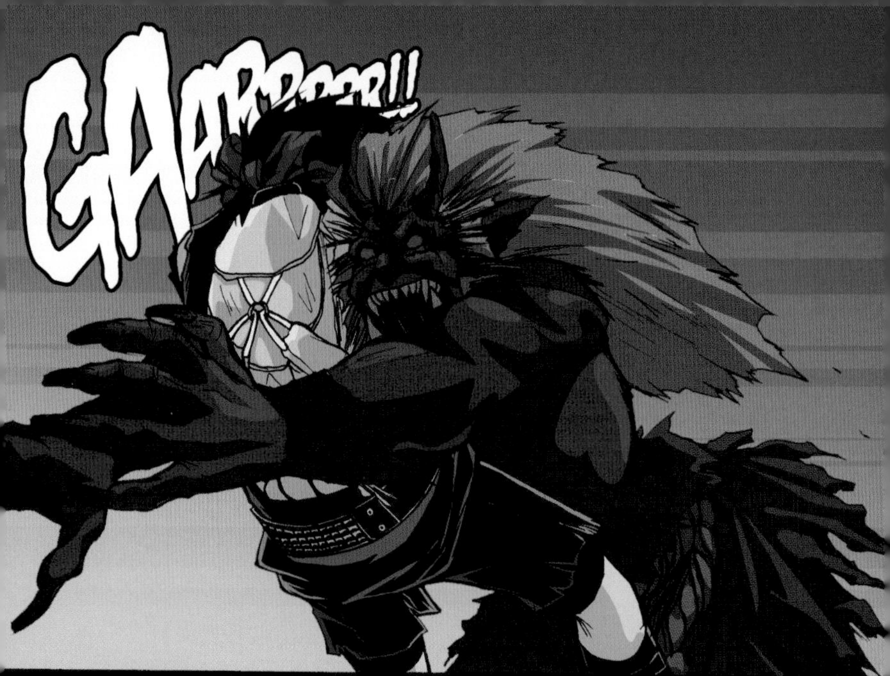
GAARRRRR!!

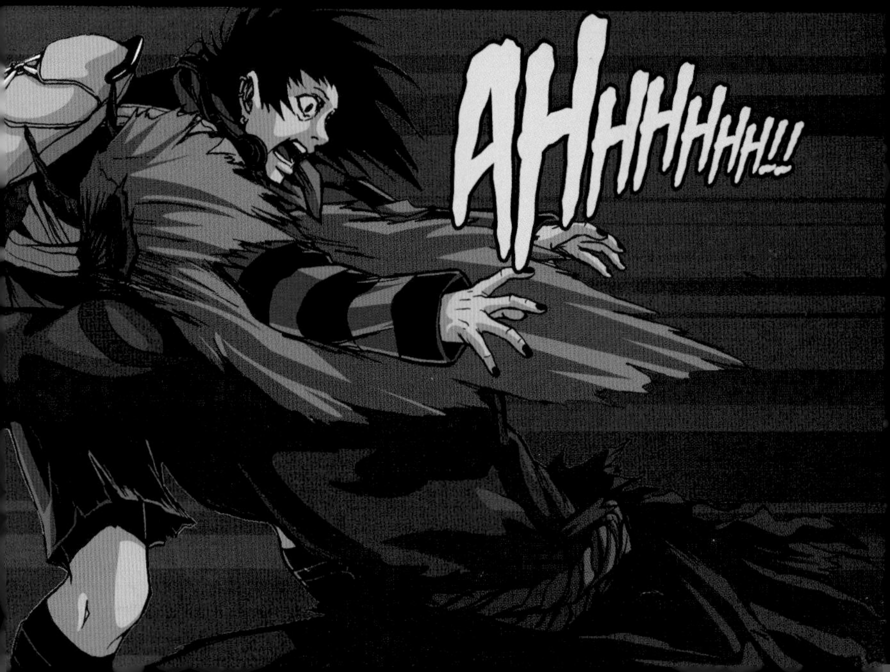
AHHHHHH!!!

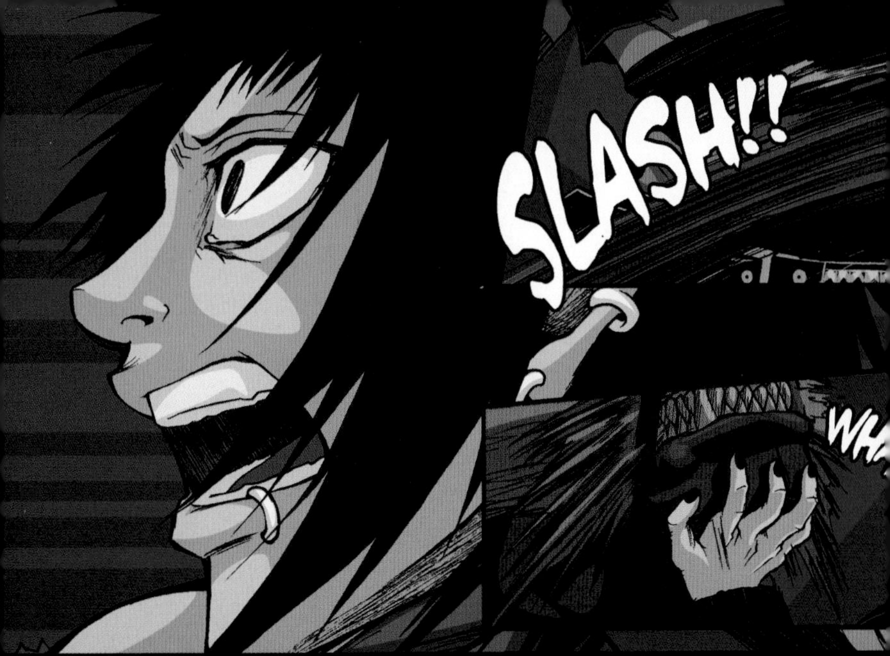
SLASH!!
WHA

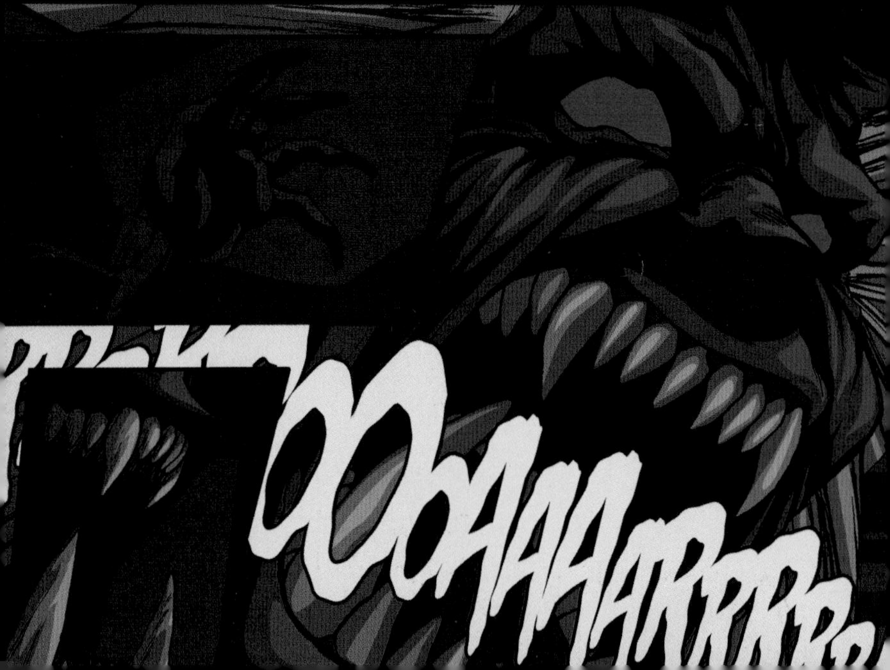
OOOAAAARRRR

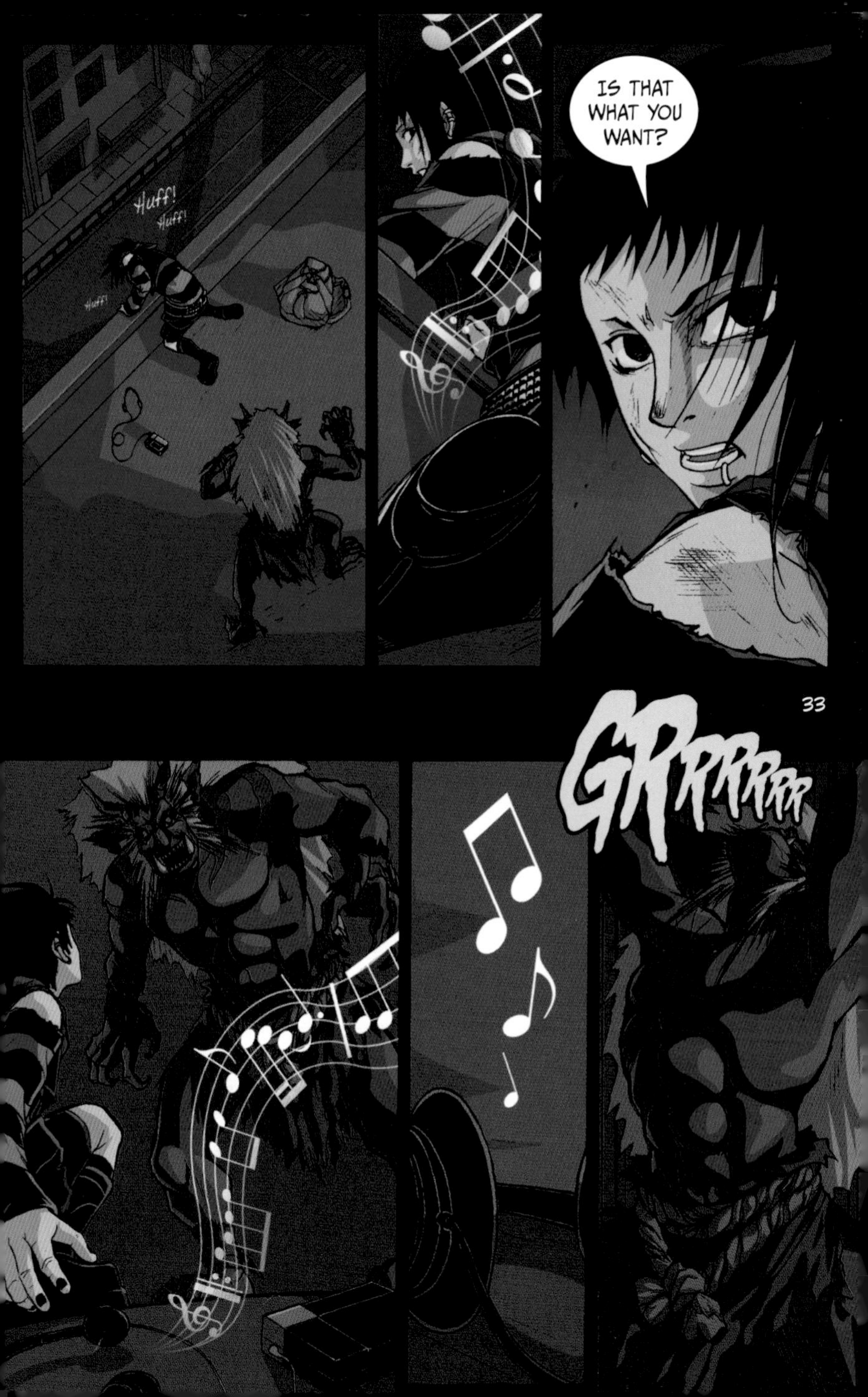
Huff!
Huff!
Huff!
IS THAT WHAT YOU WANT?
GRRRRRR

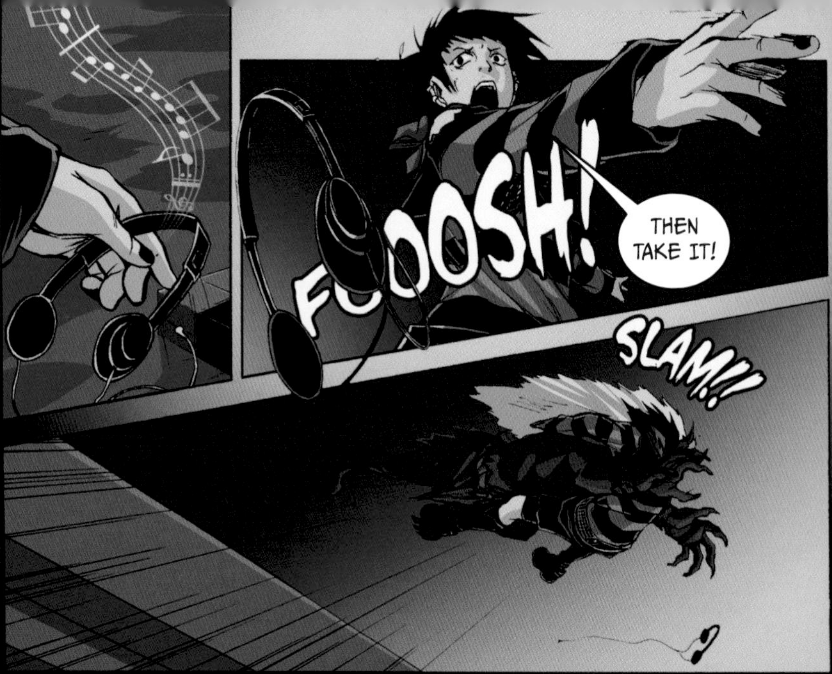
THEN TAKE IT!
FOOOSH!
SLAM!!

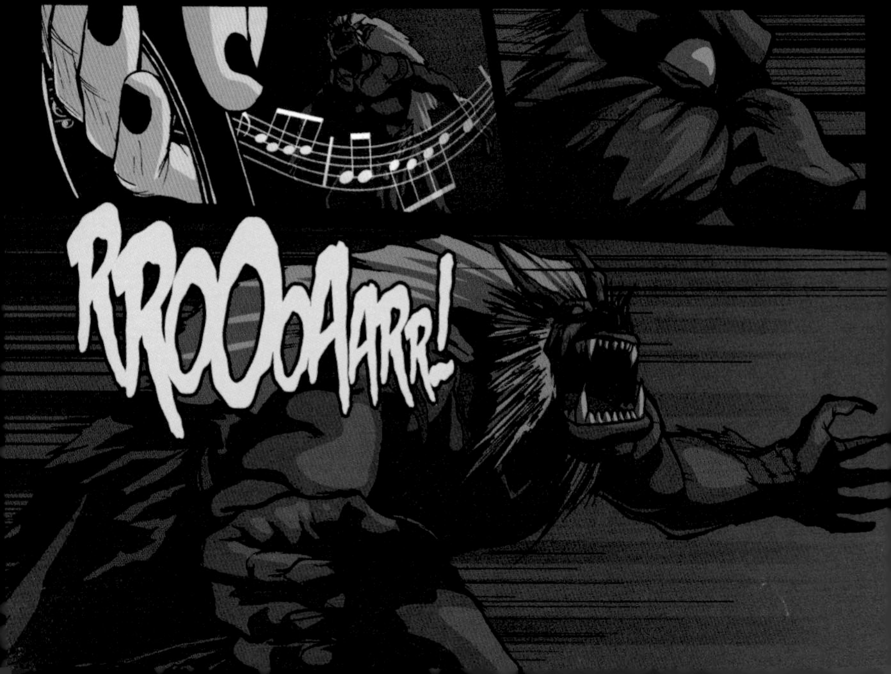
RROOOAARR!

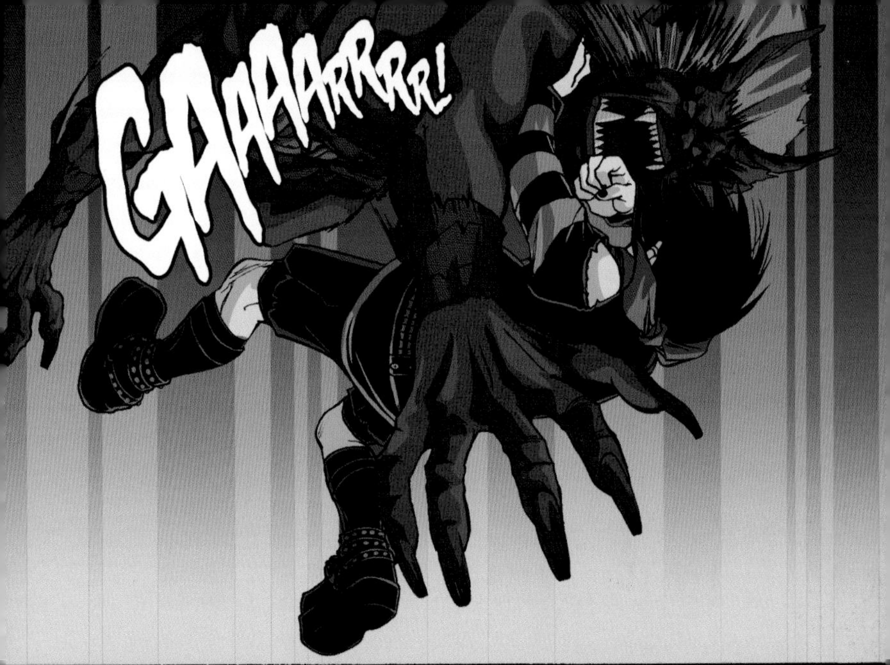
GAAARRRR!

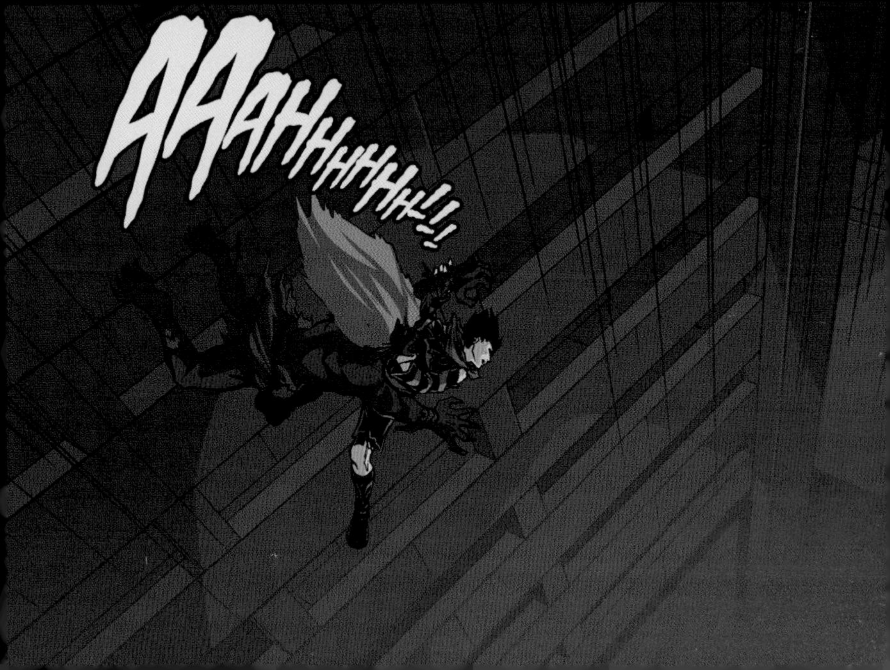
AAAHHHHHHH!!!

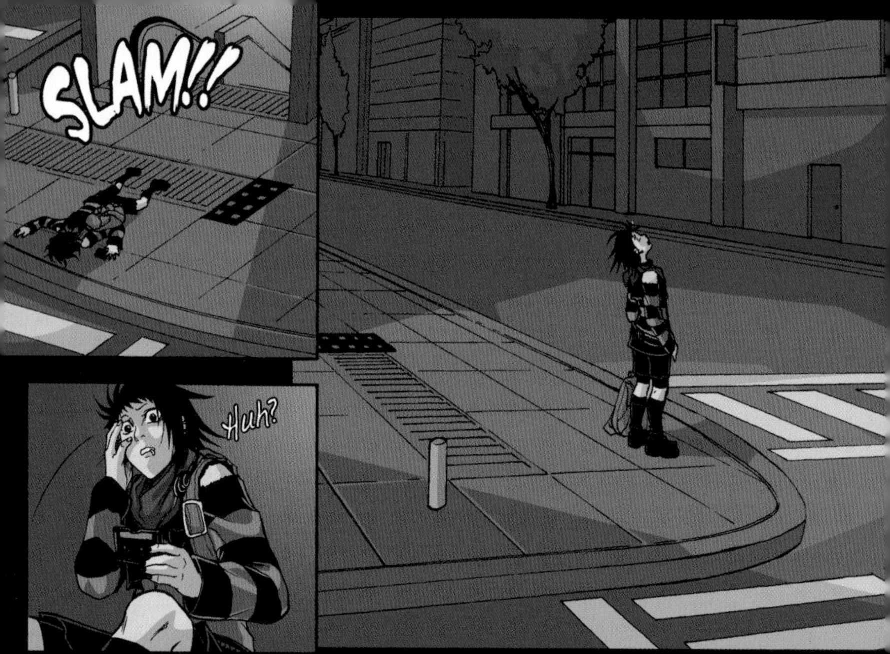
SLAM!!
Huh?

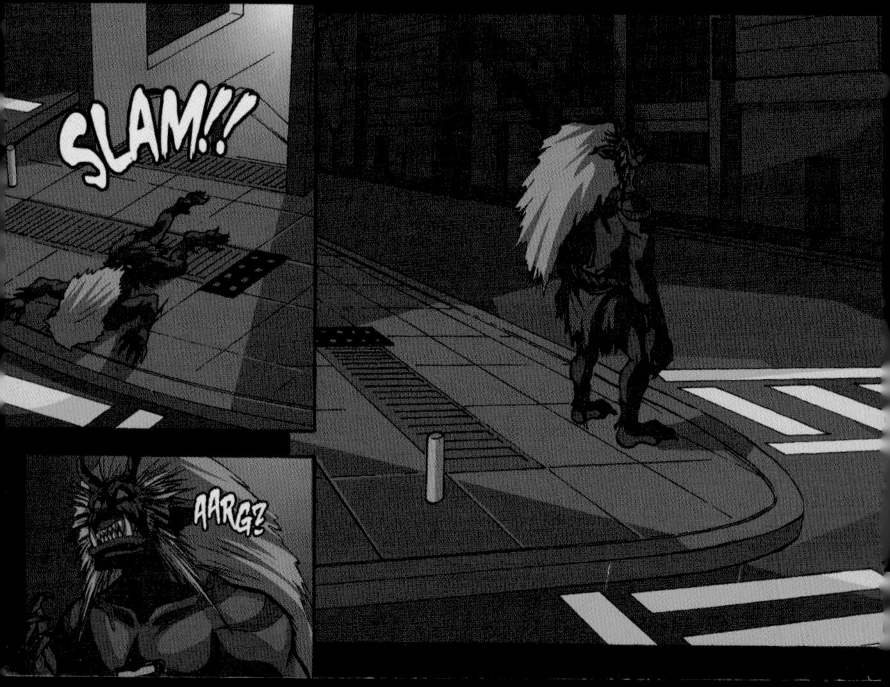
SLAM!!
AARG?

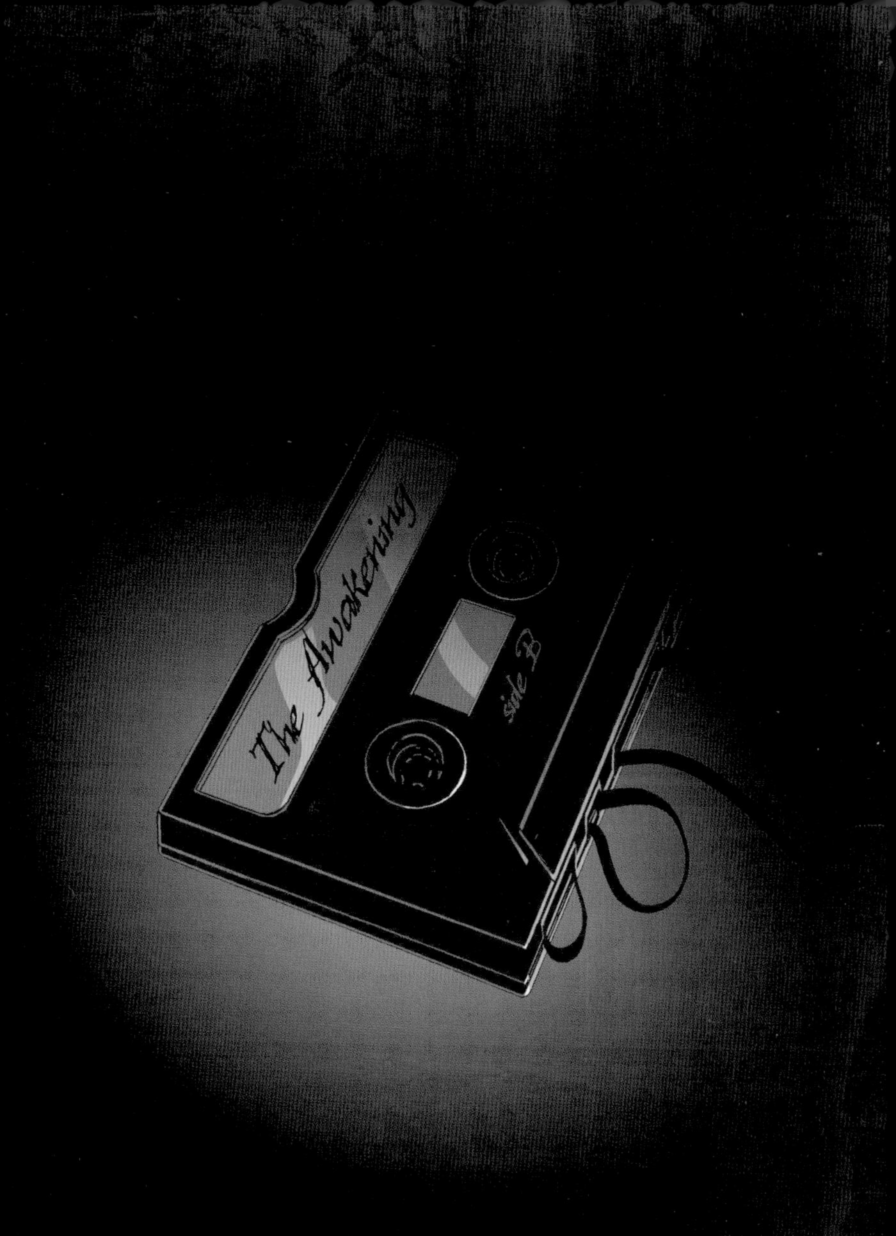
The Awakening
side B

END.

SCRIPT BY

Donald Lemke works as a children's book editor and writer in Minneapolis, Minnesota. He is the author of the Zinc Alloy graphic novel adventure series. He also wrote *Captured Off Guard*, a World War II story, and a graphic novelization of *Gulliver's Travels*, both of which were selected by the Junior Library Guild. Most recently, Lemke has written several DC Comics chapter books.

ILLUSTRATED BY

Claudia Medeiros is a freelance illustrator living and working in São Paulo, Brazil. She spent much of her childhood drawing and reading comics. Later, she trained in Japanese animation and quickly found work in Japanese comics books, also known as manga. Medeiros has illustrated several books including, most recently, *The Dark-Hunters, Vol. 1*, a manga about vampires.

VISUAL GLOSSARY

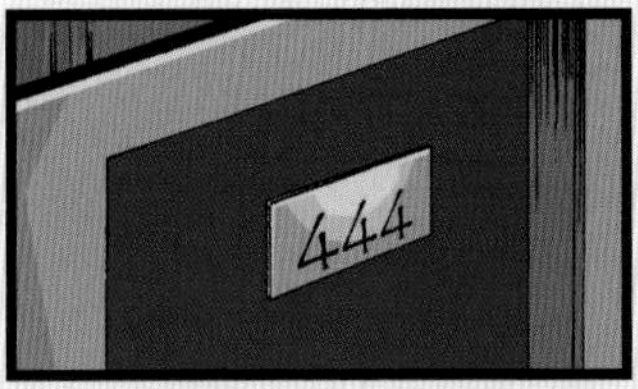
444

THE NUMBER FOUR

In Japan, some people believe this number is unlucky. The word for "four" is pronounced "shi," which has the same sound as the word for "death."

SWEAT DROPS

In Japanese comics, also called manga, artists use symbols to show emotion. A large drop of sweat often means a character is nervous or scared.

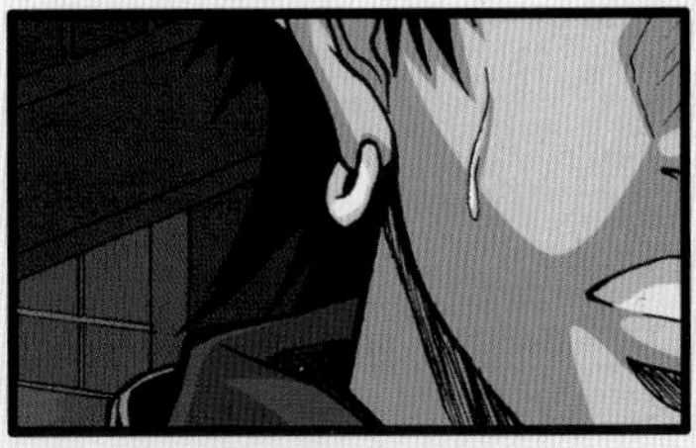

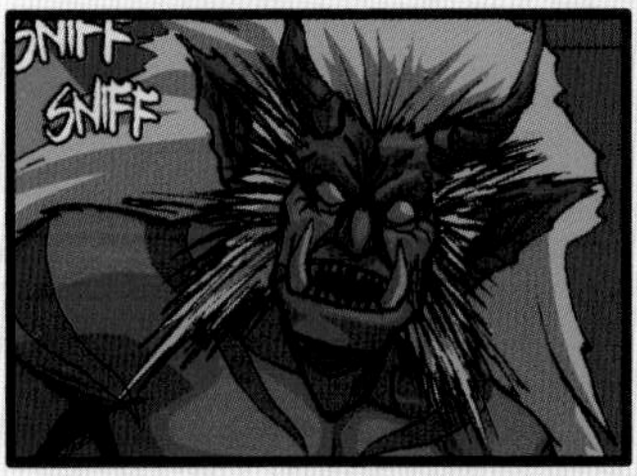
SNIFF
SNIFF

THE ONI

This ogre-like monster has been found in Japanese art and folklore for centuries. Although able to take on many forms, the oni is often a two-horned beast from the underworld.

CASSETTE PLAYER

Although rare today, a cassette player was a popular music device during the 1980s. This item helps establish an instant historical setting for the story.

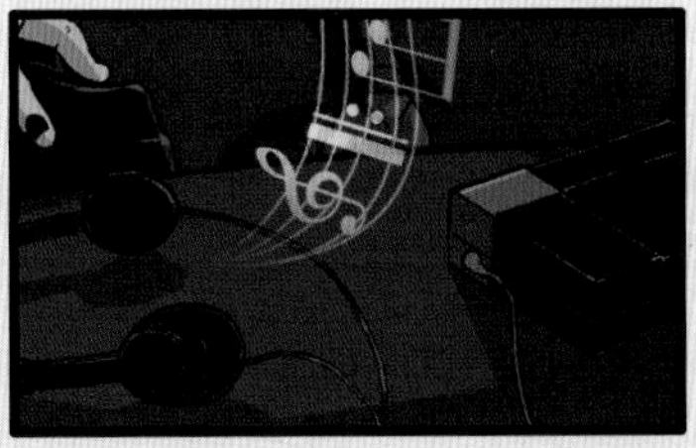

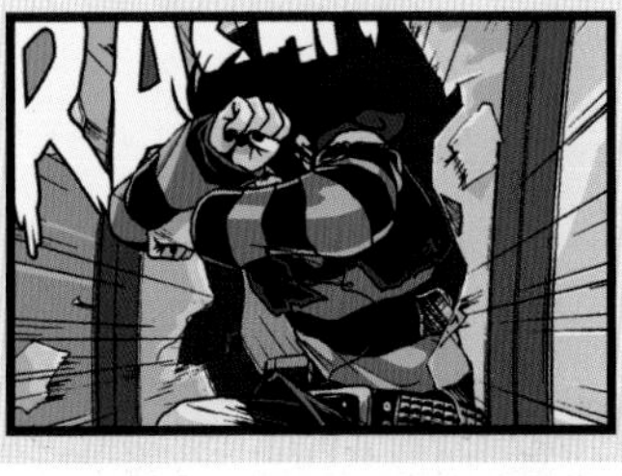

ACTION LINES

In manga, artists often illustrate sudden and fast movements, such as running, jumping, or fighting, with action lines. These dramatic lines can add speed and motion to a scene.

VISUAL QUESTIONS

1. When the Oni attacks, Yoshiro grabs a picture from the nightstand. Who do you think the people in the picture are? Explain your answer using details from the story.

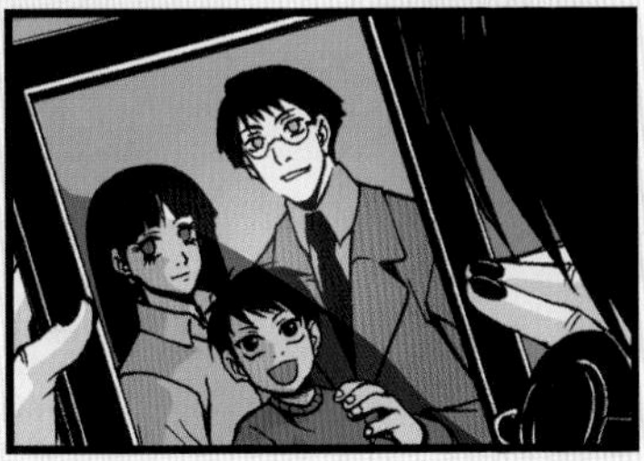

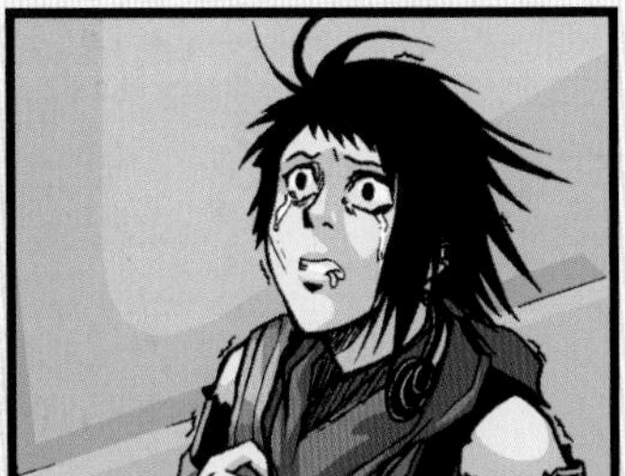

2. The way a character's eyes and mouth look, also known as their facial expression, can tell you a lot about the emotions he or she is feeling. In the image at left, how do you think Yoshiro is feeling? Use the illustration to explain your answer.

3. Yoshiro's story begins and ends in nearly the same place. Describe the similarities and differences in the images below. Why did the creators choose to start and finish the story in the same place? Do you think Yoshiro might have been dreaming the whole time? Explain.

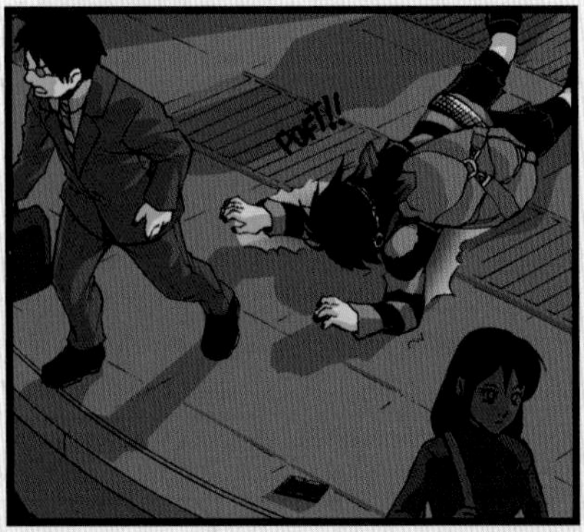
POFT!!

page 8

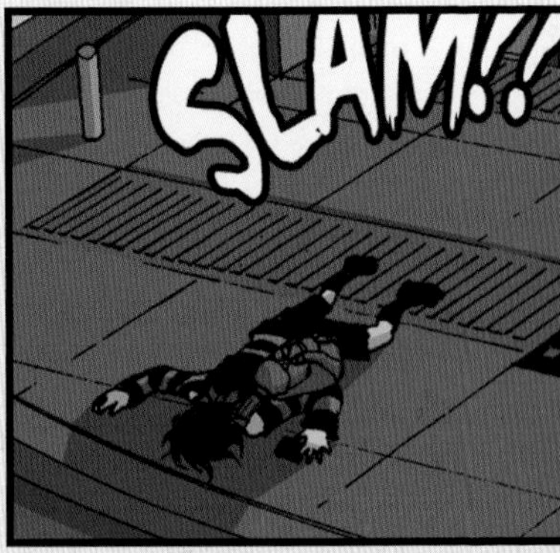
SLAM!!

page 36

4. When Yoshiro pushes Play on his cassette player, the Oni's eyes suddenly open. Do you think there is a connection between the two events? Why do you believe the Oni was awakened?

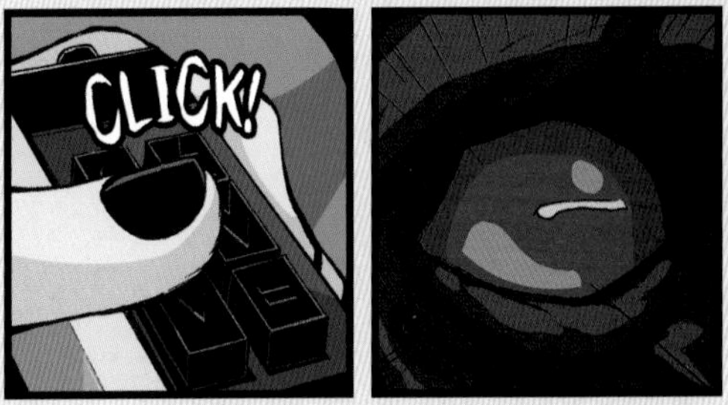
CLICK!

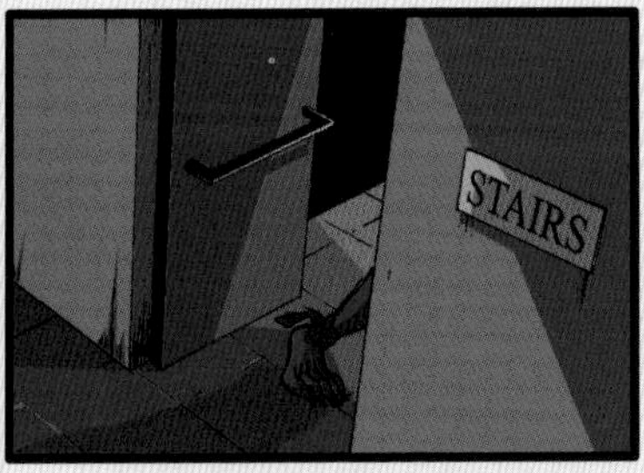
STAIRS

5. Often in graphic novels, only part of an image is needed to create an entire scene. Describe at least three things you learned about the Oni's story from the panel at left. Then write a paragraph describing what is happening.

6. The creators of this story left the ending open, allowing readers to decide what happened. What do you believe happened at the end of the story? Did Yoshiro defeat the Oni? Did the Oni and Yoshiro become one person? Explain your answer.

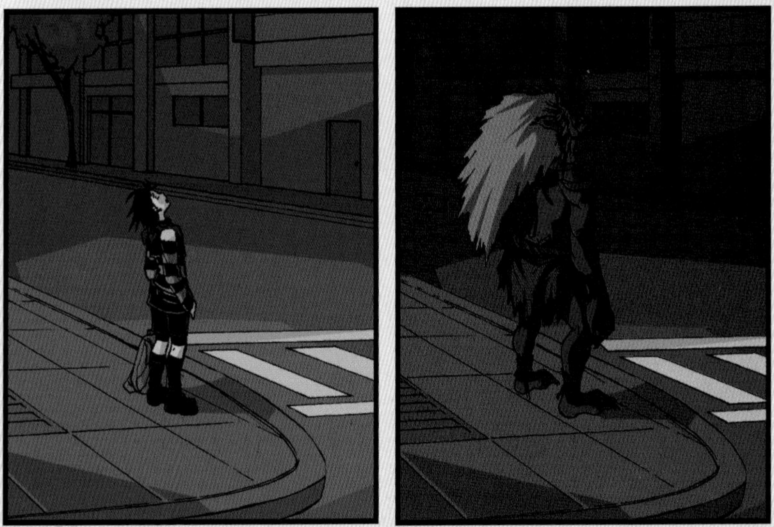

CREATING THE BOOK

THE MANUSCRIPT

Graphic novels are often created by two different people –
a writer and an illustrator. Even when a book contains few
words, the writer must provide detailed notes called "scene
descriptions," which indicate the content of each panel.

A page from *The Awakening* manuscript:

PAGE 34
Panel 1
Close on Yoshiro's hand grabbing the headphones from
the rooftop. The headphones have blue musical notes
coming out of them.

Panel 2
Medium shot of Yoshiro tossing the headphones off the
rooftop.
YOSHIRO: THEN TAKE IT!
SFX: WHOOSH!

Panel 3
Long shot of Yoshiro being tackled and pushed over the
ledge of the rooftop by the Oni creature.
SFX: SLAM!

Panel 4
Long, worm's-eye view. In the foreground, Yoshiro's
hand grabs the headphones off of the rooftop. In the
background, the Oni stands looking angry.

Panel 5
Close on the Oni's angry eyes.

Panel 6
Long shot of the Oni, claws extended and fangs exposed,
leaping into the air. Motion lines show the intensity.
SFX: GAAAAAR!!

PENCILS

After receiving the manuscript from the writer, the illustrator creates rough sketches called "pencils." The writer and editor of the book review these drawings, making sure all corrections are made before continuing to the next stage.

From page 34 of *The Awakening*:

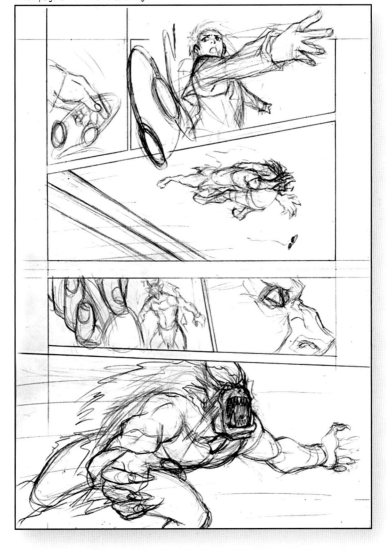

INKS

When illustrations have been approved by the editor, an artist, sometimes called an "inker," draws over the pencils in ink. This stage allows readers to see the illustration more easily in print.

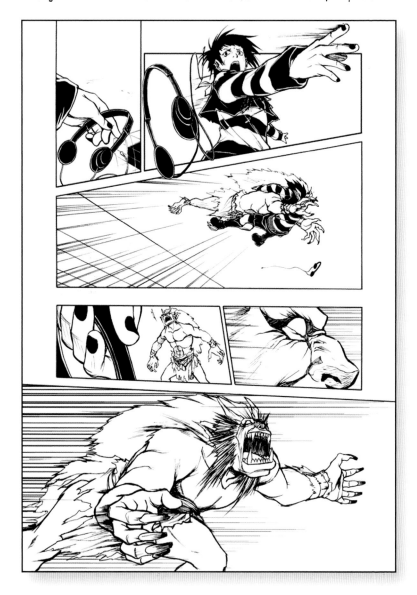

COLORS

Next, the inks are sent to a "colorist" who adds color and shading to each panel of art.

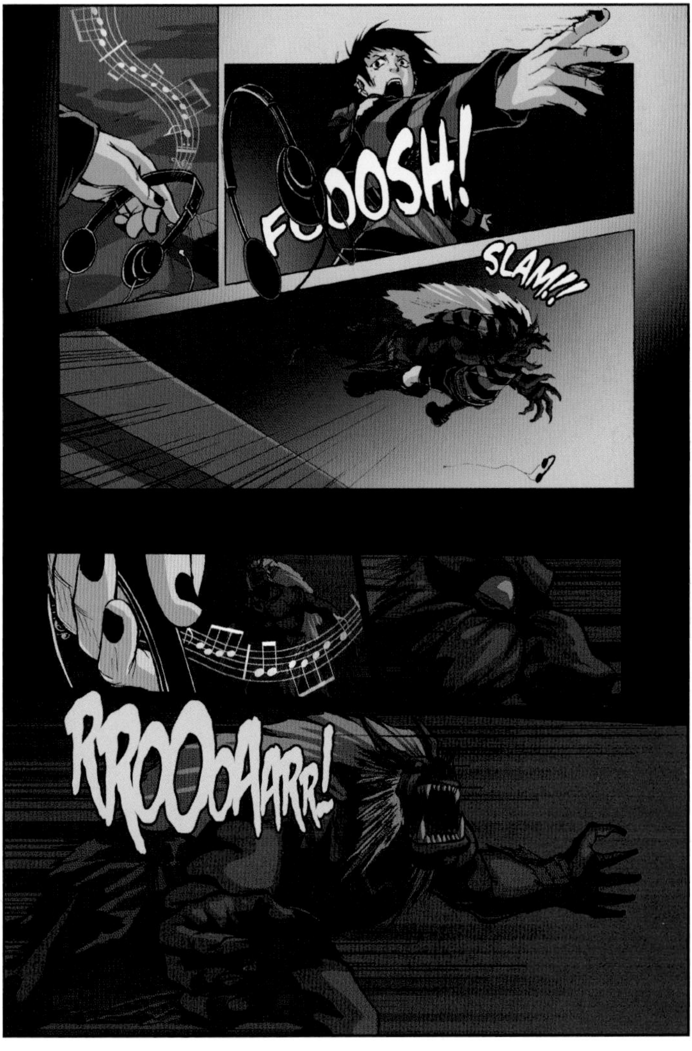
FOOOSH!
SLAM!!!
RROOOAARR!

When the art is completed, designers add the final touches, including word balloons and sound effects. Turn to page 34 to see the final version.

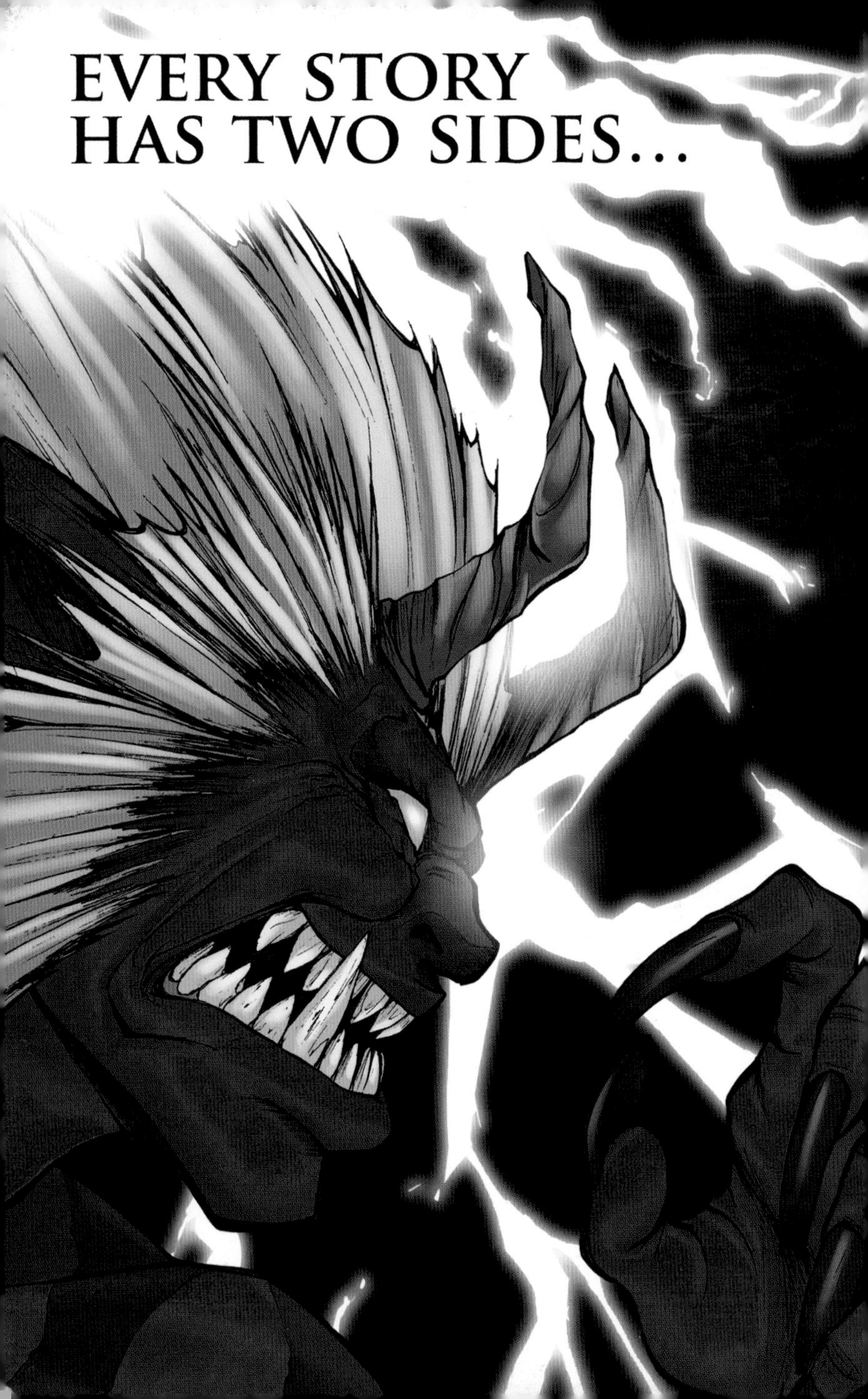
EVERY STORY
HAS TWO SIDES...

GOOD VS EVIL

Adventure

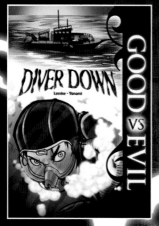

DIVER DOWN
Lemke · Yonami
GOOD VS EVIL

Fantasy

GOOD VS EVIL
DUNGEON OF SEVEN DOOMS
Dahl · Pares

Science Fiction

GOOD VS EVIL
ALIEN SNOW
Dahl · Pares

Horror

THE AWAKENING
Lemke · Medeiros
GOOD VS EVIL

COLLECT THEM ALL!

GOOD VS EVIL